W. I Chadwick

The Magic Lantern Manual

W. I Chadwick

The Magic Lantern Manual

ISBN/EAN: 9783742819758

Manufactured in Europe, USA, Canada, Australia, Japa

Cover: Foto ©Andreas Hilbeck / pixelio.de

Manufactured and distributed by brebook publishing software
(www.brebook.com)

W. I Chadwick

The Magic Lantern Manual

THE
MAGIC LANTERN
MANUAL.

(SECOND EDITION.)

BY

W. I. CHADWICK.

(Hon. Sec. Manchester Photographic Society.

WITH

ONE HUNDRED AND FIVE PRACTICAL ILLUSTRATIONS.

———

NEW YORK:

SCOVILL MANUFACTURING COMPANY,

423 Broome Street,

W. IRVING ADAMS, Agent.

1886.

PREFACE TO THE SECOND EDITION.

THE writer hopes to be acquitted of presuming to teach many new things to his brother lanternists by this little treatise; he is actuated rather by other motives in giving a few practical explanations and descriptions of the various forms of Magic Lanterns, with their details and application; and although forming a book of instruction to the learner, he trusts it will take its place as a handbook to the expert lanternist.

In the inquiry for a New Edition of this little work, opportunity has been taken to subject the whole matter to close scrutiny and revision, and, consequent upon the development of this particular subject, it has been found necessary to make such additions as is thought sufficient to cover any new ground up to date.

W. I. CHADWICK.

Eccles, near Manchester,
March 27th, 1885.

CONTENTS.

————✦✦————

THE MAGIC LANTERN MANUAL.

INTRODUCTION.

SO much has previously been said and written on the value and merits of the Magic Lantern as an instrument for instruction and amusement, that the author does not think it possible to add much interest by enlarging upon what is already known. But for the benefit of those readers who may not have studied the Magic Lantern, it may be remarked that within the last ten years this instrument has become much more popular than for some time previous. By the introduction of the "Sciopticon" there is little doubt that a new interest was awakened—that instrument admirably filling up the wide gap between the old-fashioned oil-lit lantern and the more elaborate oxy-hydrogen instrument, about all of which something will be said by-and-bye. More recently a keener interest still has been developed, as, by the introduction of the gelatine process of photography, the number of amateur photographers in this country has been more than doubled. The photographer soon discovers that there is no more enjoyable way of exhibiting his productions, and reciting the pleasures of his rambles, than by means of his lantern.

Many different ways of applying the Magic Lantern present themselves, perhaps none more pleasing than its adaptation to Dissolving Views, which were invented by Mr. Child, the method of their production being long kept a secret by him. These charming effects were then produced as now, viz., by two lanterns provided with suitable arrangements for gradually cutting off the picture of one lantern, and disclosing that of the other by alternately shutting out the light from each lantern. Ever since their introduction they have formed an everlasting source of amusement and instruction at many scientific institutions throughout the country. To give some idea of the public appreciation of such exhibitions when properly conducted, it may be stated that at an exhibition of photographs of statuary given in this way at the Manchester Mechanics' Institution some years ago, over seven hundred pounds were realized in a few weeks.

The popularity of the instrument has increased by its use to the photographer for enlarging purposes, and in many other ways its utility, combined with photography, has of late placed it as an indispensable apparatus to the science teacher, &c.

The simplification of oxygen gas-making for the lime light lantern has also played its part by placing powerful lights in the hands of almost inexperienced persons, with whom the manufacture of oxygen gas, in the old form, was a dreaded affair, and one only to be read about. However, these fears are now of the past, and exhibitions by the oxy-hydrogen lime light may now be conducted on from 20 to 30 feet screens with almost as little trouble and risk of accident as with the ordinary oil light. This has only to become more widely known to again multiply our lanternists, and let us hope that before long every schoolmaster and educational teacher may be possessed of one or other form of this useful instrument.

Perhaps nothing could have enlivened the spirit of lantern exhibitions so much as photography, for now we are able to procure at a cheap rate photographic slides of almost every country in the world, and these, as well as being arranged in series, can be obtained with excellent descriptive lectures accompanying the different sets.

Of late years photographic dry plates, the extreme of simplicity in preparation, have been brought to a high state of perfection, and the whole manipulation reduced to simple rules, so that every tourist may become a photographer.

Cameras and apparatus have also had the careful consideration of both home and foreign makers, the result being that cameras for pictures up to stereoscopic and cabinet size, not exceeding one pound in weight, may be carried in the pocket, with a stand for holding same in the portable form of a walking-stick, umbrella, or alpenstock. So that a tourist may set off on his travels with his photographic apparatus in his pocket, and may return with thirty or forty souvenirs of places visited without the inconvenience of extra luggage. Thus holiday rambles may be by the aid of photography illustrated and described, and continental tours be made the subject of enjoyable and everlasting reminiscences, reproduced by aid of the lantern to our friends at home with almost living majesty.

Lectures and slides upon astronomy, natural philosophy, and in fact most other branches of science and art, are to be purchased already arranged. Temperance tales, fairy tales, comic stories, and lessons for the young are obtainable (either by purchase or hire), and still our producers' lists are not complete, and a boundless ocean is open to those who are willing to embark in the buoyant ship Industry, navigated by Captain Perseverance and his honoured crew, with Fortune at the helm.

THE MAGIC LANTERN.

THE Magic Lantern of to-day is in principle the same as constructed by Kircher about the sixteenth century, and described by him in his book "*Ars magna lucis et umbræ*," although it would appear that Cellini must have used some such instrument a century previous to produce phantom figures in the smoke of a fire.

The principal arrangements of the instrument consist of an illuminating power (Fig. 1), with a lens called a condenser (C) placed between the light and the picture (s). In front of this latter is placed another lens, styled an objective (o). A light-tight box encloses the whole, and prevents the emission of light, except through the lenses above mentioned.

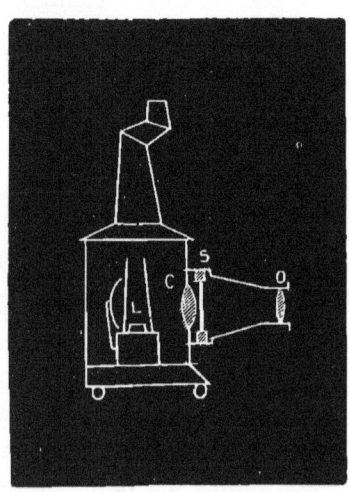

Fig. 1.

It will be perhaps as well, before entering into the illuminating powers and various forms of lanterns, to describe the optical portions of the arrangement.

OPTICAL ARRANGEMENTS.

The Condenser is for the purpose of collecting as many of the rays of light as possible, and transmitting them through the picture on to the screen. This being understood, we will now consider the best form and size for our requirements. There are differences of opinion as to the best form of condenser for the Magic Lantern. At this there is no need for surprise, as the writer has frequently heard lanternists expressing opinions in matters concerning the optical arrangements, although possessed of but a very imperfect optical knowledge, and in some cases ignorant of the object of the various arrangements. One of the most primitive forms of condensers is the simple plano-convex lens, or common bull's-eye. This collects a certain quantity of light on the one side and distributes it on the other (the convex side); but as these "bull's-eyes" are never of short focus, they require to be farther from the light, and thus the angle of illuminating power collected is small. For it will be shown that in two condensers of unequal foci—maintaining the same diameter—the angle of light collected by each separately would differ in proportion to the square of the distance between the light and the condensers : thus, a 4-inch condenser, 5 inches distant from the light, would only receive one-fourth the light that it would if placed 2½ inches distant. But in shortening the focus of the condenser we are limited, by reason of its necessary additional thickness, which increases its liability to fracture, being placed nearer to the light. The shorter the focal length of the lens the thicker it must be, consequently more liable to come to grief.

Double condensers are therefore better adapted for our present requirements, for if two such lenses as above described be placed together, the focal length of the combination is reduced one-half, so that a double condenser of 3 inches focus can be made by placing two lenses each of 6 inches focus together. As such lenses would be proportionately thinner, they are more able to withstand the heat to which they are sometimes subjected.

Different arrangements of double condensers have from time to time been tried, with the object of taking in a greater angle of light, and of being as free from spherical and chromatic aberration as possible (consistent with moderation in cost). The nearest combination of these qualities (all of which are a desideratum in a good condenser) will be found in one introduced by Sir John Herschel in the year 1821. This is generally considered to be about the best double condenser, and the one most generally adopted in good lanterns.

It consists of a meniscus and a bi-convex lens mounted together, with the concave side of the meniscus next to the light (see Fig 2).

 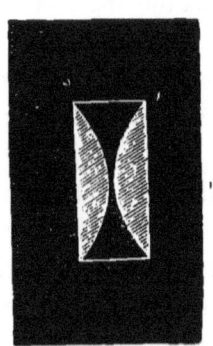

Fig. 2.   *Fig.* 3.

In purchasing, notice should be paid to this point, as the author has several times found in lanterns of a supposed first-class character that the lenses of the condensers were mounted the *wrong way*—viz., the concave side nearest the picture, and the bi-convex side next the light. How this should have happened he is at a loss to conceive, unless it be that those employed in putting lanterns together either know no better or have not given the matter consideration. He was much surprised a short time ago to receive from a celebrated maker a pair of condensers which were mounted the wrong way, and upon inquiring into the mistake, the reply was that the lenses were in the positions as usually supplied to the shops.

Another form of double condenser, which has been extensively used during the last few years, consists of two plano-convex lenses, mounted with their convex sides together, almost touching (Fig. 3); and although for all ordinary purposes there is no choice between this and the last described, yet this one has the advantage of being produced at a somewhat cheaper rate. As a superior condenser the triple form carries the palm. There are many modifications of this style, the first of which the author believes was constructed by the late Mr. Andrew Ross, in 1836; but he believes the most approved to be that recommended by Mr. J. Trail Taylor, in the " British Journal Photographic Almanac," 1877, consisting of

a pair of lenses mounted similar to Herschel's arrangement, with a small plano-convex lens interposed between them and the light, as shown in Fig. 4. By this arrangement the focus is shortened, and a greater angle of light collected. The introduction of a small plano-convex lens may also be adapted to the double plano-convex form (Fig. 3), and it was by the use of this arrange-

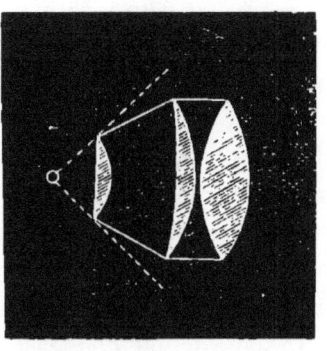

Fig. 4.

ment some years ago that the illuminating power of the old lanterns at the Royal Polytechnic, with large long-focus condensers, was greatly increased.

Triple condensers are often used in lanterns of American manufacture of the best quality, and although they do not seem to be so generally adopted in this country as they merit, the author has every confidence in recommending them to those in search of the best condensers. The size of condenser must, to some extent, be decided by the size of picture to be shown, as for small pictures it is useless to have large condensers, throwing rays of light, only a portion of which are transmitted through the picture.

In the days of hand-painted slides, which were usually of large size (in some instances as much as 6 inches square or more), condensers of equal proportions were necessary to cover them; but now that photography has stepped in, we are able to produce slides of small size with much greater delicacy and finer detail than is possible for our ablest artists to produce on large size slides; consequently, having reduced the size of our pictures, we may proportionately reduce the size of our condensers.

Should the pictures be square or cushion-shaped (the case in most French slides, as well as in those of our American cousins, and also of many produced by the Woodbury process), a condenser must be used a little larger in diameter than the diagonal distance across the picture; but with slides mounted in circles (as those of Mr. York and others) smaller condensers may be used. For general purposes, the author has concluded that condensers having a diameter of 4 inches, and a focus of 2½ to 3 inches, are the most useful size, this diameter being large enough to cover the largest photographic slides in general use.

In some double condensers each lens is made of different quality of glass, and this has misled some to suppose that they were achromatic. It is not necessary that the condensers should be perfectly achromatic, and it is preferable that all condenser lenses should be composed of the whitest flint glass.

Although a few specks, bubbles, or even a scratch or two, are not very detrimental to a condenser's performance, such would not be offered by any optician of standing. Let care be taken that the lenses do not fit too tightly in their mounts, so as to allow for expansion by heat when in operation; they should be sufficiently slack to be turned round in their cells by the fingers.

Before using the condenser it is advisable to warm the same before the fire or otherwise, so that the sudden heat when the light is turned up may not fracture it, also to dispel any moisture that may accumulate on the lenses. An outlet for this moisture should be provided in the centre of the brass ring in which the lenses are mounted, by having a few holes drilled therein.

OBJECTIVES.

Having fully described the condenser and its functions, let us now consider the matter of the Objective Lens. Its duty is, to magnify the small picture previously illuminated by aid of the condenser, and to project the same on to the screen.

The qualities desired in a Lantern Objective are equal definition at sides and centre of picture, depth of focus, freedom from distortion and from chromatism. Although it is of importance to adopt condensers of good construction and quality, it is of far greater importance that good object glasses be used; for, with a condenser of somewhat inferior quality, and a good Objective, a much better result will be obtained than could be with a good condenser and an inferior Objective. The author would not, therefore, feel justified in occupying time or attention in describing the worst of all Objectives—a single bi-convex lens, used only in inferior or toy lanterns. Better than this are two plano-convex lenses, mounted with the convex sides together, similar to the condenser (Fig. 3); but, to get anything like good definition, they must be of long focus; and in "second-rate" lanterns, this is often objected to, they being principally used for showing comic slips, where the larger the picture the better appreciated by the juveniles.   Some lanternists pride themselves upon the large size of disc they can show, and often it is required to exhibit a picture 10 feet in diameter in a distance of 10 feet; but, as short-focus lenses disperse the rays of light at greater angles, inferior definition is the result. A short-focus Objective, which has found favour with many, consists of a bi-convex and a meniscus lens mounted together : the bi-convex being nearest to the picture, and the concave side of the meniscus outside, or farthest from the picture, with a diaphragm a little distance in front of it.   Although giving better definition than those previously mentioned, the small diaphragm, which is necessary to give sharpness to the picture alike at centre with edges, tends to diminish the illumination on the screen.

The Photographic Portrait Combination Lens possesses all the requirements necessary in a Lantern Objective; for while being achromatic, it has, if of moderately good quality, sufficient depth of definition and flatness of field to satisfy the most fastidious.

These lenses have received the careful consideration of many of our ablest opticians, and, by reason of their extensive manufacture, they can be procured at an exceedingly low price.

An Achromatic Portrait Combination is made by Darlot, and also by many English makers, of moderately short focus ; and although the front lenses are of less diameter than the back combinations, the screws are made alike, so that the front lenses can be reversed, and thereby a long-focus Objective obtained, which in many instances proves a great convenience, as when working from the back of an audience in a large room.

It must be remembered that when working with the single long focus lens a diaphragm should be used in front.

In the best lanterns at present made lenses of various foci are supplied, usually of $7\frac{1}{2}$, $9\frac{1}{2}$, and 12-inch focus, the tubes being telescopic and capable of extension to the necessary requirements of the lenses used. This is often found more convenient of adaptation to the various sized rooms in which such exhibitions are conducted.

For his own choice, the author much prefers to see a small, sharp, bright picture, than a large one of inferior definition and illumination; therefore, for this reason, would recommend the adoption of Objectives of long foci, whenever it may be practicable.

It must be understood that the smaller the picture is shown the brighter will be the illumination, for "light decreases inversely as the square of the distance;" thus, a picture shown to 10 feet in diameter would be about twice as well illuminated as if shown 14 feet diameter, or exactly four times as well as if shown 20 feet in diameter.

An approximate rule, which will be found useful and sufficiently correct for all practical purposes when it is necessary to determine the lantern's distance from the screen, to produce a certain disc with a given lens, can be best obtained as shown by the formulas below :—

Size of opening in slide in inches = S
Focus of Objective in inches = F
Lantern distance from screen in feet = L
Diameter of disc in feet = D

$$L = \frac{D \times F}{S}, \qquad D = \frac{L \times S}{F}, \qquad F = \frac{L \times S}{D}$$

The following examples will probably make this more clear :—

Suppose we wish to find the distance at which to fix the lantern from the screen, to produce a 15-feet disc with a 6-inch lens, using a 3-inch slide. We multiply the diameter of disc D by focus of lens F, and divide by size of slide S, which will give us the distance, viz., 30 feet.

We will now imagine a case where, in a certain room, we must work our lanterns from a gallery, or upon a screen at an unalterable distance, possessing only one lens ; we should naturally wish to know the size of disc we could produce. To arrive at this we must multiply lantern distance from screen L by size of picture S, and divide by focus of lens F. Another illustration will complete our series.

As in the previous instance, the distance at which we can work our lanterns from the screen is fixed, and also the diameter of the disc is a settled matter, and we wish to know the focus of the lens it will be necessary to use ; therefore, by multiplying L by S, and dividing by D, the answer will give the focal length of lens required.

Having now completed our survey, and described the optical portions of the Magic Lantern and their respective functions, let us now, describe and illustrate the various illuminating powers applicable.

The simplest form of these is the little ordinary oil-lamp, now only used in toy lanterns, which throw a disc of 2 to 4 feet, for exhibiting comic slips.

Superior to this is the "Argand Fountain Lamp," with concave silvered reflector (shown at Fig. 5), in which circular wicks and the best sperm or colza oil can be used, previously camphorated. It may be comphorated by adding camphor, previously pounded in a mortar, with a little alcohol, about one ounce to the pint of oil being sufficient. It has been recommended to soak the wicks in strong vinegar, and allow them to dry thoroughly before use, as a preventive against charring.

Reflectors should be of the same focal length as the condensers, the illuminating power being directly midway between the condenser and the reflector. Often no attention is paid to this matter, the result being that the reflector is worse than useless. Glass reflectors, when silvered by Liebig's process (on the surface, not behind), are much superior to metal ones. We must not omit to mention the Argand Burner, in which house gas is used as adapted

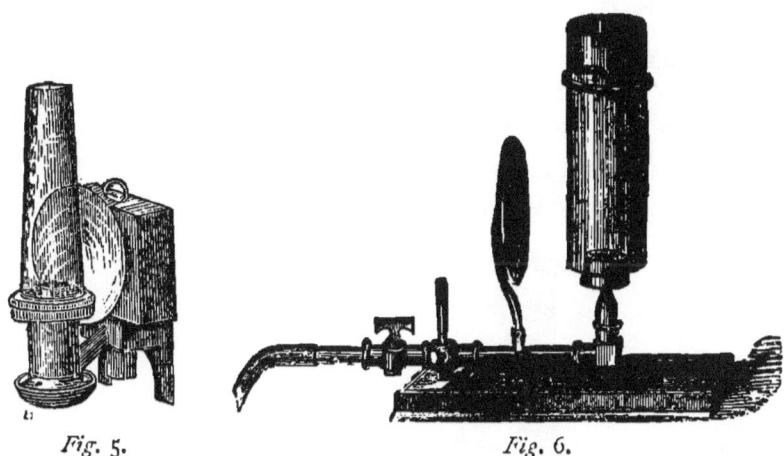

Fig. 5.   *Fig.* 6.

to the Magic Lantern (Fig. 6). It has an advantage in cleanliness, and sometimes in convenience; but its illuminating power is inferior to the oil lamp, and is only suitable for exhibiting comic slips on small screens. The "Silber Lamp," though it surpasses those previously mentioned in illuminating power, falls far behind that of the "Sciopticon," which it will be now our duty to describe.

THE SCIOPTICON.

THE name of this instrument is equally novel as is its whole construction, when compared with the original instrument. The name is derived from two Greek words signifying " Shadow

View" or "Shadow Picture." Its inventor is Mr. L. Marcy, of Philadelphia, and it was first introduced into this country by Mr. W. B. Woodbury, who thought it a fit instrument to institute as a medium between the old oil lantern and the expensive and elaborate oxy-hydrogen lantern.

Its chief feature is its lamp, which is arranged to use two wicks, placed edgewise to the condenser, and in which paraffin or the best crystal oil (camphorated as previously explained, but in less quantity) may be used to produce a light far surpassing anything previously seen in the form of oil lamps.

Its optical portions are of exceedingly good quality, and its

Fig. 7.

convenient and novel form, together with its lightness and portability, have secured for it an unexceptionable reputation. Fig. 7 shows an external view of the instrument, and Fig 8 is a sectional view of the same, by which we will explain its various parts.

A B C and D are the lenses of the achromatic objective, E the milled head for focussing, F the flange of the objective, by which it is secured to the ring G, which is made of wood, for the convenience of changing the objectives for any other size or description that may be necessary in a special case. H and H', framework carrying objective, which is made to draw in or out to suit the focal length of the objective. L, portion of framework forming base of the instrument. M and N, claw and flange, by which the instrument is secured to the top of a neat packing-box, with which it is supplied. o and o', stage and spring for the reception of slides and pictures : this is of a most convenient form, allowing the top

Fig. 8.

to be open for the introduction and manipulation of chemical, photographic, and other scientific experiments. P Q, the condenser lenses, 4 inches in diameter, and of short focal length, mounted on a very approved plan, which permits of either lens being removed from its cell. s, the lamp reservoir, of sufficient capacity to hold, when full, enough oil for four hours' entertainment. It is not advisable to fill this reservoir too full, and care should be taken not to allow any oil to get outside, in which case an unpleasant smell is sometimes produced. u and v, tubes carrying 1½-inch wicks, each of which are disconnected in their length, thus preventing the transmission of heat from the flame to the oil-chamber, and by keeping the oil quite cool, avoids any objectionable odour. w w, buttons for adjusting the wicks. e e′, interior of flame-chamber. g g′, are a pair of glasses closing the ends of the flame-chamber; their liability to fracture has been entirely overcome by using toughened glass. h, concave silvered reflector, also used to close the back of the instrument. i and j, chimney and cap, which are made telescopic, and can be taken off for convenience of packing.

The merits of such a powerful oil lantern must be apparent to all. One objection has been raised to it, namely, that of a slight shadow crossing the illuminated disc, in a vertical direction; but this is of so little consideration, that when a picture is being shown it is not perceptible, except with such slides as show a great amount of sky, and in this case it can be reduced to a minimum by a proper attention to the wicks. Other modifications of double-wicked lanterns have been introduced, but it cannot be said with much improvement. One of these was to contract the wicks at the front ends, and to expand them at the back, to obviate the seeming defect of the dark line above mentioned; but after considerable experience with one of this class, the author found that by this placing of the wicks out of parallel, the flame was more likely to "fork" and the wicks to burn unevenly, and after some time a portion of the illumination was sacrificed.

Other forms of both double and triple-wicked lamps have since been introduced. The one styled the "Patent Refulgent Lamp" is constructed both with double and triple wicks, and possesses merits in many ways, which go to prove its excellence.

Since the introduction of the Sciopticon, many improvements have been made by the Sciopticon company and other firms. The lamps are now made detached from the body of the lantern, and in the new Sciopticon Lamp a circular glass is used at each end of the flame-chamber, they having been found to withstand the heat better by reason of their equal expansion and contraction, and their liability to break thereby considerably reduced.

One of the valuable improvements of Mr. Newton was the

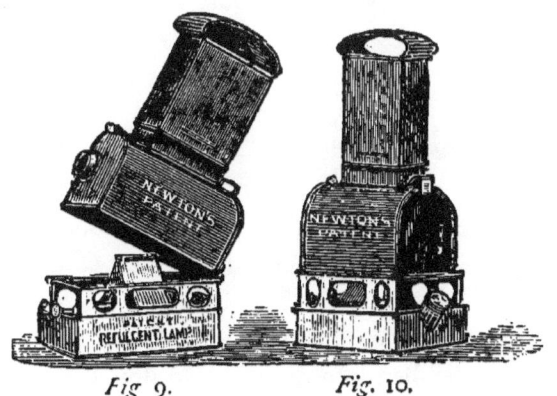

Fig 9.   *Fig.* 10.

introduction of a hinged-silvered reflector, closing the back end of the flame chamber. In the centre of this reflector is a small, blue glass window, through which the flame may be viewed to adjust the flames (see Figs. 9 and 10).

Various other forms of oil-burning lamps are now in the market, some with three and four, and another with five wicks. One styled the "Pamphongos" is stated to give a very superior light; but the writer's recent experience with one of the most modern

5-wick lamps brings him to conclude that the extreme delicacy and attention necessary in the adjustment of the wicks to prevent smoking and the great amount of heat emitted are serious drawbacks.

The Sciopticon, and most other oil-burning lanterns, are now adapted so that limelight can be introduced.   Having now completed our review of the family of oil-burning lanterns, it may be well, before entering into a description of the Oxy-Hydrogen Limelight, to allude to other lights which have from time to time been tried with more or less success.

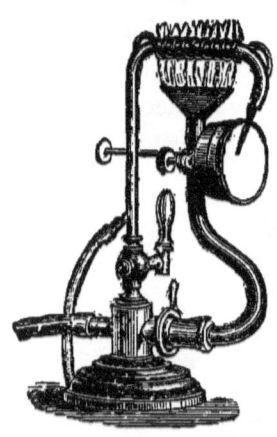

Fig. 11.

The Pyro - Hydrogen Lamp (Fig. 11) was some few years ago introduced into this country from Germany by Mr. Walter B. Woodbury.   The light was produced by a jet of heated air blowing at a high pressure through a flame of hydrogen, and projected upon a disc of lime.   The light was inferior to the oxy-hydrogen in its poorest form, and the trouble nearly the same, and has for the present fallen into disuse.   No doubt the idea will, at some future time, receive further attention, and may possibly develope into a more practical means of illumination.

THE MAGNESIUM LANTERN.

A S an illuminating power the combustion of the metal magnesium must not be omitted. As adapted to the Magic Lantern its success has been limited, principally owing to the unsteadiness of the light, and to the necessity of providing a long

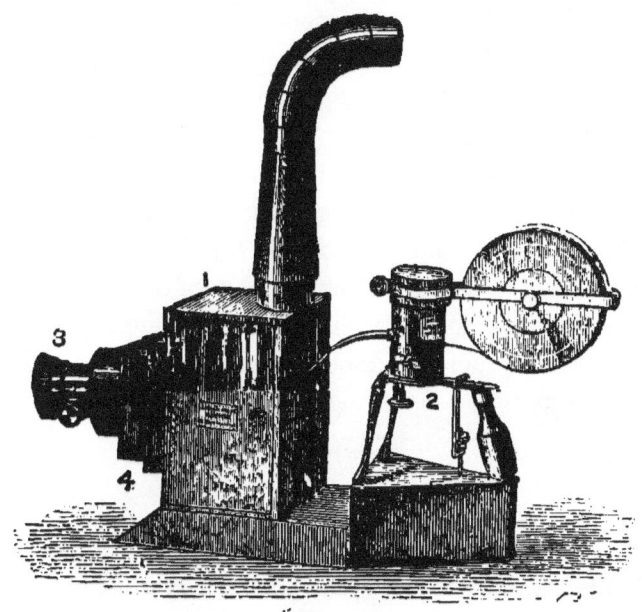

Fig. 12.

chimney to carry away the great amount of magnesia vapour, the result of the combustion. For these and other reasons it is not used for Magic Lanterns generally, but may be adopted in the case of a lecturer or experimentalist wishing, during his lecture, to show an occasional diagram. The most practical apparatus of this kind is, perhaps, that manufactured by Mr. Solomon, constructed to burn the metal in ribbon or wire form, and is fitted with an ingenious clockwork arrangement for self-feeding. The arrangement of lamp and lanterns are clearly shown at Fig. 12.

Besides the aforenamed lamp, there was, some years ago, another in the market, invented by a Mr. Larkin, constructed to burn the magnesium in the form of a powder, which was obtained at a much cheaper rate. And although this lamp possessed very great merit, it was probably abandoned before being brought to a practical issue, and it must be regretted that such a beautifully actinic and powerful light as magnesium has not been yet brought into more general use, and, for anyone having the time and opportunity to devote to its serious consideration, there is a field open here for bringing to the aid of the lantern what must always be regarded as a most valuable adjunct. Probably the present high price of magnesium has precluded the introduction of other appliances for its combustion, but no doubt this would be materially altered by the application of such a method as would bring magnesium into greater demand.

THE ELECTRIC LIGHT.

WITHIN the last few years the Electric Light has been applied to the lantern in a variety of forms, with more or less success. In the best forms the light is superior to the lime light, but its unsteadiness, and the great liability of the lamps not working, and its cost of maintenance, has placed it far behind the lime light for general purposes. In such institutions as the Victoria University (Owen's College), Manchester, under the able management and superintendence of Sir Henry Roscoe, it is used chiefly for scientific demonstrations and research.

THE LIME LIGHT.

THE "Lime Light," or, as it is sometimes styled, the "Drummond Light," has been in use as far back as the year 1820. It consists of a jet of oxygen blown through a flame of hydrogen on to a piece of lime, which latter is rendered so extremely incandescent, that a light is obtained superior in importance to any, the electric excepted. Sometimes the flame of a spirit lamp is substituted for that of the hydrogen; it is then known as the "Oxy-Calcium Lime Light." Before proceeding to enter upon the different methods of using the gases, it will perhaps be as well to explain the mode of their manufacture.

OXYGEN GAS.

Where the manufacure of oxygen gas, not only for illuminating purposes, but for sanitary purposes also, is conducted on a large scale commercially, the method of M. Tessié de Motay is usually adopted. Briefly described, it consists in heating in a large retort manganate of soda, and blowing through it high-pressure steam, which carries with it the oxygen contained in the manganate of soda. After all the gas has been extracted, the steam is shut off, and air is introduced to the retort, which restores to the manganate of soda the oxygen in place of that which had been extracted. It is then subjected again to the steam jet, and so on with steam and air alternately, the manganate of soda being always replenished with oxygen on the admission of the atmosphere. A large manufactory on this principle was established at Brussels, as also in many of the large cities in America, where oxygen gas is produced as cheaply as 25s. per 1,000 cubic feet.

In England the making of oxygen gas is usually conducted on

a small scale, consumers having generally to prepare their own ; but it is to be hoped that ere long we may be blessed with similar advantages, and have the opportunity of purchasing oxygen gas at a rate somewhat proportional with that of house gas. There are various other methods of producing oxygen gas than the one above described, but as our object in this treatise is to produce in quantities suitable for lantern requirements, it is only necessary to speak of the most practical and economical methods of arriving at this result.

From one pound of chlorate of potash in the form of crystals or powder, to which one-third of a pound of black oxide of manganese has been added, together heated in a retort, four cubic feet of oxygen gas may be obtained, although theoretically there should be more. The exact proportion of this mixture is not of importance, as the manganese undergoes no chemical change under the operation, the oxygen being wholly derived from the chlorate of potash, which, if used alone, would liquefy on the application of heat, and give off the gas so quickly as to be ungovernable. The addition of the manganese is merely to separate the particles of the chlorate, so that the gas when given off may be more under control ; also by its addition less temperature is required. After all the oxygen has been given off, the residue is chloride of potassium and oxide of manganese : the former being soluble in water, may be separated from the latter by decantation, and after drying may be used again and again with an assurance of its purity. The greatest care must be exercised in the purchase of these chemical ingredients, as the introduction of any organic matter into the retort on heating, the same would ignite, and a serious explosion would be the inevitable result. Some years ago an acquaintance of the writer's, who in the exercise of his profession had made this gas a thousand times, one day upon being called upon for a bag of gas, found his stock of manganese exhausted, he therefore sent out to a neighbouring chemist's shop for a supply. By some means the manganese had been accidently mixed with soot, which in appearance it somewhat resembles, and on using some a fatal accident resulted. Although it is very rarely that manganese is intentionally adulterated, it is well to be on the safe side, and safety from such accidents as the one alluded to may be obtained by heating the manganese to redness in a crucible before mixing it with the chlorate of potash. This is a simple matter, and should be done with every fresh sample. By reason of its small cost it may be purchased in sufficient quantity to last a season. (Chlorate of potash can be purchased at from 7*d.* to 9*d.* per lb., and manganese at 2*d.* per lb.) Care must also be taken that no deleterious substance enters during the roasting. If desired, fine sand may be substituted instead of manganese, but it must be previously rid of any organic matter.

Retorts best suited to oxygen-making are those made of sheet iron, conical in shape and brazed together, having a dish bottom and a brass top, on to which latter is attached by screws a loose brass cap with a piece of bent wrought iron tube screwed therein.

As a medium for making the joint between the retort and the cap, the writer advocates "asbestos," which is very durable and effective.

The gas in passing from the retort (if to be stored in a bag) should pass through a wash-bottle, sometimes called a "cooler" or "purifier," consisting of a "Woulff's Bottle" partly filled with water. The tube connecting the retort with the wash-bottle may be partly of lead and partly of india-rubber, the leaden portion being of sufficient length to reach nearly to the bottom of the bottle, and should be perforated with small holes at some dis-

tance from its end, thus forming a rose-head.   The gas in passing
through the water will be purified, cooled, and rid of any particles
of manganese, which are sometimes carried away with the gas from
the retort, and which are apt to choke the nozzles of the jet if the
washing be omitted.   The outlet-pipe should be a bent tube long

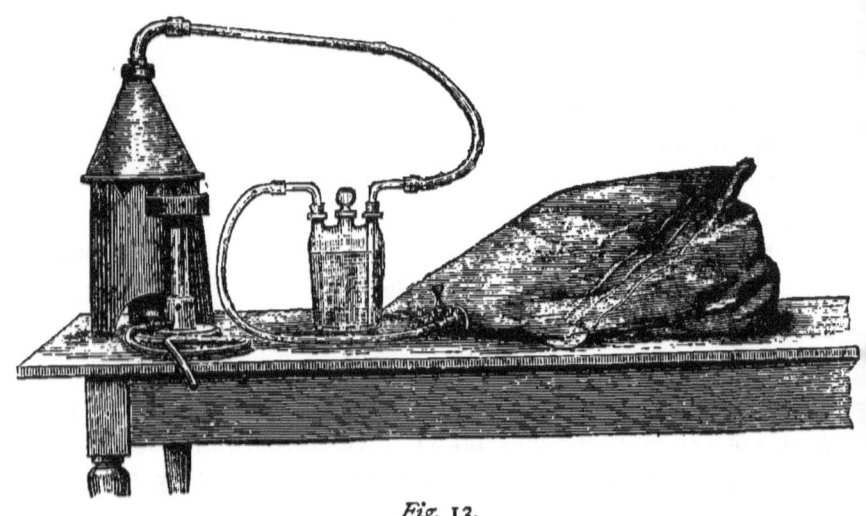

Fig. 13.

enough to enter the bottle, and sufficient in length to connect with
the gas-bag.   The whole arrangement is illustrated at Fig. 13.

   The retort may be heated on a fire, or by gas, which latter is
preferable, a large Bunsen burner being placed in the conical
stand, which is of sheet iron, and forms a support for the retort.
The Bunsen burner has been shown out of position to illustrate
the kind adopted.   Though this is a matter upon which the reader
may use his own discretion, many of the burners, made by Mr.
Thomas Fletcher, of Warrington, for cooking and other uses,
being admirably suited to the purpose.

So soon as the gas has been given off (which may be noticed by the cessation of bubbling in the wash-bottle), the tube connecting the retort with the wash-bottle should be disconnected; if this be neglected, and the heat from the retort withdrawn, a vacuum will be caused on cooling, which may draw the water from the wash-bottle into the retort, and a miniature boiler explosion will very likely be the result. To obviate this, an empty bottle may be placed in the tube between retort and wash-bottle; thus in the case

Fig. 14.

of a vacuum being created, the water in the wash-bottle would be simply drawn as far as the empty bottle, without proceeding farther (see Fig. 14).

It may be well here to remark that before proceeding to fill a bag with either oxygen or hydrogen, it should be warmed to soften it; and any old gas it may contain should be expelled by folding and rolling up the bag.

HYDROGEN GAS.

It is beyond doubt that pure hydrogen is superior, in illumination, as compared with house gas (carburetted hydrogen). Not only is less of it required, but also less oxygen to produce an equal result, though the trouble of making it does not always repay the advantages gained. In most large towns in this country a fair pressure of house gas can be had, and for ordinary lantern exhibitions this is used direct from the main in what is called a "safety" or "blow-through jet." When the

pressure is feeble, as it usually is in small towns, it is custo-
mary to fill a gas-bag from the main, and to use it under pressure,
in the same way as the oxygen. Hydrogen gas is produced by
the action of dilute sulphuric acid upon zinc; the gas being
liberated and sulphate of zinc being deposited. At Fig. 15 is

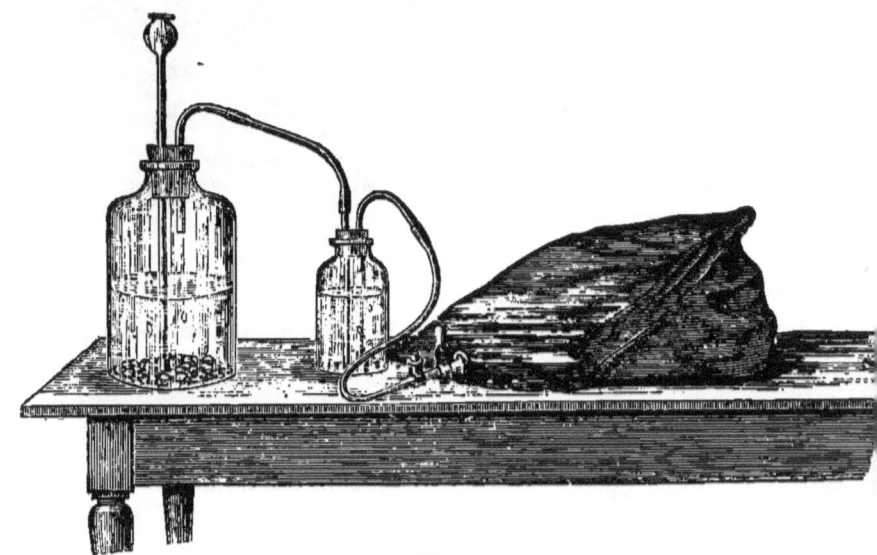

Fig. 15.

shown a general arrangement for the purpose of making this gas.
It consists of a glass bottle, with a good tight-fitting cork, and a
funnel-top tube extending nearly to the bottom of the bottle,
through which the sulphuric acid and water (in the proportion of
6 of water to 1 of acid) are poured, and thus brought into contact
with granulated or clean zinc cuttings lying at the bottom of the
bottle. The gas should be allowed to blow through for a short
time to get rid of the air contained in the bottle at starting, and
then may be collected by the bent tube from the upper portion of

the vessel. If the gas is to be used from a bag, it should be washed in like manner as the oxygen, as shown in the en, graving.

Döbereiner's Lamp (Fig. 16) is an automatic hydrogen genera- tor, and may be made of large size if re- quired. A is a glass cylinder containing a very dilute solution of sulphuric acid; z is a small block of zinc suspended by a lead wire inside the glass funnel F, which is cemented to the top E, and closed by the stop-cock C. By action of the acid upon the zinc, F is soon filled up with gas, dis- placing the solution, which is driven into A, and thereby stopping the action. As soon as the stop-cock is opened the hydrogen is liberated, through a jet, on to a piece of spongy platinum, which produces a light.

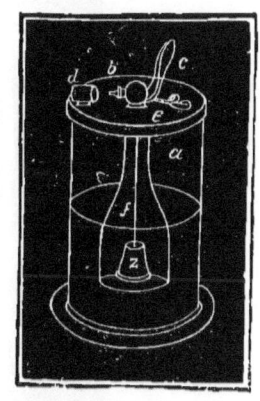

Fig. 16.

As the hydrogen is liberated the solution will rise in F, and the action is immediately renewed between the acid and the zinc, and continues so long as the stop-cock remains open.

Many modifications of this apparatus have been devised: one by the author is illustrated at Fig. 17. It was constructed of two large earthenware jars, the top jar having the bottom cut out, and it was fixed in an inverted position over the bottom one by a good deep india-rubber stopper, made of a block of india-rubber, fitting each jar-mouth tightly, and through which a lead tube passed to the bottom of the under jar. Upon this lead tube was fixed a cylinder of zinc. The outlet pipe was also a leaden tube secured into the india-rubber stopper. The apparatus was charged by fill- ing the bottom jar with sulphuric acid one part, and water six or seven parts; then by connecting the upper jar the gas was quickly

generated, and the liquid forced up the leaden tube into the upper
jar.   A steady pressure could be maintained with this apparatus,

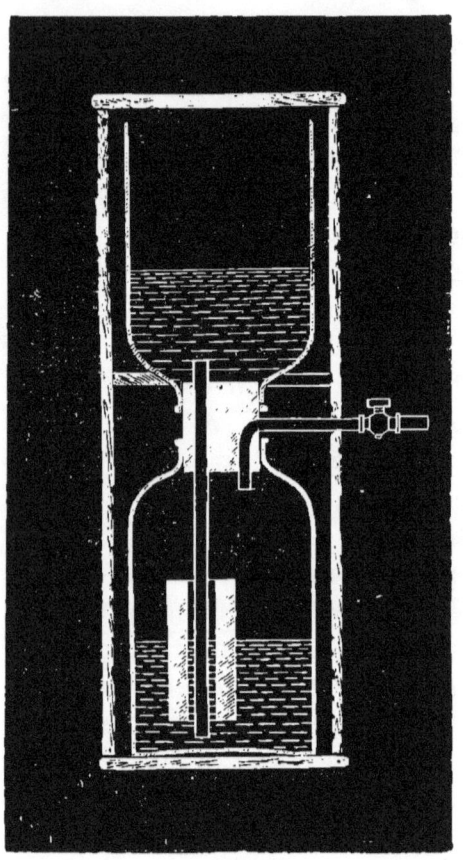

Fig. 17.

which was wholly enclosed in a neat wooden box with a loose
top and front.

LIMES.

Limes for use with the oxy-hydrogen light may be purchased in
two forms and of two kinds and qualities—namely, discs and

cylinders, hard and soft, and *good* and *bad*. Shape is of little importance; the one most in general use and perhaps most convenient is cylindrical, about 1 inch in diameter and $1\frac{1}{2}$ inches long, perforated in their entire length with a hole $\frac{3}{16}$ inch in diameter to fix them on to the lime-pin of the jet. Discs are made of two sizes, $1\frac{3}{4}$ and $2\frac{1}{2}$ inches in diameter. Hard limes are found best suited for the oxy-hydrogen and high pressures, soft ones being best for oxy-calcium and low pressures. Those known to opticians as "Excelsiors" are perhaps the best in the market, and answer well for any form of Lime Light.

As lime has a powerful affinity for moisture, and will not keep intact if exposed to the atmosphere, it is necessary to wrap them in tinfoil after they are made, and pack them in an air-tight box or bottle large enough to contain a dozen. An excellent plan for preservation is to dip them in a solution of india-rubber in benzole.

In whatever form the limes are preserved, as a preventive from splitting when the oxygen is turned on, they should be thoroughly dried before use. A good plan is, upon taking them from their box, to place them in the oven or on the top bar of the fire-grate until they are quite hot.

It is not an unfrequent occurrence, and one not a little annoying, to find upon opening a box of limes that moisture has gained admittance, and that the limes are slacked and worthless. Many substitutes for lime have been tried with more or less success; the best of these which has come under the author's notice being the oxide of zirconium, which is described by Du Mothay as "the most infusible, unalterable, and the most luminous substance at present known."

Many years ago the author purchased an oxy-hydrogen lamp of French manufacture, in which a small piece of oxide of zirconium was used instead of lime, but he found that it was not so imperishable as it had been represented. By the continuous action of the oxy-hydrogen flame for a few hours it decreased materially in size; however, it was a step in the right direction.

Artificial limes have previously been described and made by many lanternists, and to this subject the writer has devoted considerable time and expense, with the object of producing an efficient substitute for the crude lime; and within the last few months has renewed his research in this direction, conjointly with Mr. Lewis Wright, subjecting zirconium and other substances to a pressure of 90 tons to the square inch, and, though the results of these experiments have not been thoroughly successful, it is hoped at some future time these and similar experiments may be renewed, trusting to find, at all, events, a better substitute for lime than that with which we are at present acquainted.

It is as well to possess a few artificial limes in case of emergency, and for the lecturer who may only require a light occasionally, perhaps the best for such a purpose is made of

Precipitated chalk .   .   .   .   . 8 parts.

Carbonate of magnesia (ponderous)   . 1 „

mixed together, with the addition of a little very thin gum water, and subjected to a good pressure.

In preference to purchasing, many make their own limes, which can be done from a block of unslaked lime, to be obtained at almost any town in the kingdom.

GAS-BAGS.

These have been the receptacles in most general use for the gases used in lime-light effects. They are made of mackintosh cloth in the form of a wedge, and of two qualities, the best being made of three thicknesses of cloth, with india-rubber inserted, of black material generally, and are in the end by far the cheapest

and most serviceable. When out of use, all the old gas should be
expelled, and may be folded up and put away. Sometimes they
are liable to become somewhat stiff; this can easily be removed
by warming for a short time before a fire or placing them for an
hour so in a warm room.

For those who may by accident chance to have a leaky gas-bag,
it is well to mention an excellent remedy, which in all cases of
emergency will prove effectual. This is a piece of common sticking-
plaster made hot and applied. The author has known this method

Fig. 18.

to be used in cases where india-rubber solution has been out of
reach, and it has answered admirably until a better remedy could
be applied.

When both a bag for oxygen and one for hydrogen are used,
they must be kept for their own respective gases, and not inter-
changed, each being marked O or H to signify their contents; therefore, whenever a bag is to be filled, all old gas and air should be
expelled by folding the bag with the tap open, and before unfolding
the bag the tap should be closed, to prevent any air being sucked

back. As soon as the connections are made the tap can be opened. When bags have to be transported or sent by rail, it is a good plan to have a loose outer covering of canvas or similar material.

PRESSURE BOARDS

Are necessary with gas-bags, to form a means of applying weights. They consist of two boards hinged together at one end, with a semicircular hole cut in same end to allow the pipe and tap to project. A hinged shelf is usually fixed on the top board, upon which the weights are placed (see Fig. 18). This is the best form of pressure board, being a lever, with the fulcrum at the hinges.

Fig. 19.

Sometimes a single board is used, which is fixed by hooks placed in the floor at the lower end of the board.

When using both oxygen and hydrogen from gas-bags it is of

the utmost importance to have the pressures equal. With this object a pressure frame has been devised to contain two bags, which
latter must be the equal size on the surface presented to the pressure frame, though it is not necessary that they should be of equal
depth ; thus the hydrogen bag may be deeper in the wedge form
than the Oxygen bag, seeing that more of the hydrogen is used.

Only one set of weights are required, and if the above precau-
tions have been attended to, the pressure on both bags will be
alike, as will be seen by Fig 19. This frame is composed of
wood, with canvas inserted, and by straps at the back the bags
are prevented from slipping. Weights are rarely ever included in
a travelling lanternist's outfit, being generally obtainable in some
form or other everywhere.

The weight necessary to give sufficient pressure on large bags
for oxy-hydrogen mixed gases is as much as two hundredweight
and sometimes more, but with safety jets and oxy-calcium half this
amount is usually sufficient. Although the method of gas-bags
and pressure boards is excellent so far as portability goes, it has
the failing of inconstancy of pressure, also the wear and tear is
great. For fixed or permanent use, gas-holders are highly preferable.

INDIA-RUBBER TUBES.

The best quality are those of a red colour, and when cost is not
considered, those of extra thickness of walls are most suitable, as
they do not so suddenly bend or kink, and close the passage. The
author purchased some of this class, which it is almost impossible
to block up in the passage by bending. Large-bore tubes are
preferable to the small-bore ones we see so generally used, and if
of any great length, should be at least ½ inch internal diameter.
It is astonishing how small a reduction in the passage will reduce
the pressure considerably. Tubes should not be used that are in-

ternally lapped with iron wire, as the wire reduces the pressure by friction.   In the coupling of tubes, see that the couplings are as large in the bore as the tube : often this is not the case, but the coupling is the same diameter outside as the tube is inside.   An easy method of coupling is to turn the tube inside out for an inch or so, then insert the coupling and pull the tube back again to its original form.

All taps should be looked to, to see that there is a full and free passage through them, as not unfrequently the plug is bored with a hole not one-half the area of the tube.   It is, therefore, always desirable to use taps of a size larger, with the plugs well cleaned out and lubricated with tallow.

GAS-HOLDERS.

Where the lime light is often required in one fixed place, gas-holders claim many advantages over gas-bags. No wash-bottles are required ; the gas does not deteriorate in quality by being stored ; and, if properly constructed, one even pressure can be maintained ; none of which advantages are to be derived from gas-bags and pressure boards.   Gas-holders are sometimes made of zinc, but more frequently of iron.   A friend of the author's has a very good and useful one fixed in his garden, and made of two casks, the outer one being sunk into the ground, and the inner one inverted, forming the holder.   For a cheap article this is a very effective one, although not very elegant in appearance.

The best gas-holders that have come under the author's notice were two constructed for a friend.   They were made in shape similar to a small dish-end steam boiler, of wrought iron plates $\frac{1}{8}$-inch thick, well riveted together.   A man-hole was cut, and a cover for same attached (as in a steam boiler), by which a boy could get inside to clean out and paint when necessary.   A cut of same will be seen at Fig. 20. The pressure was applied by water from a cistern, and conveyed to the inside of the holder by the pipe P. The end of this pipe was covered with a small quantity of water placed in a cup, open at the top, and from this cup another pipe takes the overflow to the bottom of the holder, so as to avoid the splashing and noise. The amount of pressure is regulated by the distance between the surface of the water in

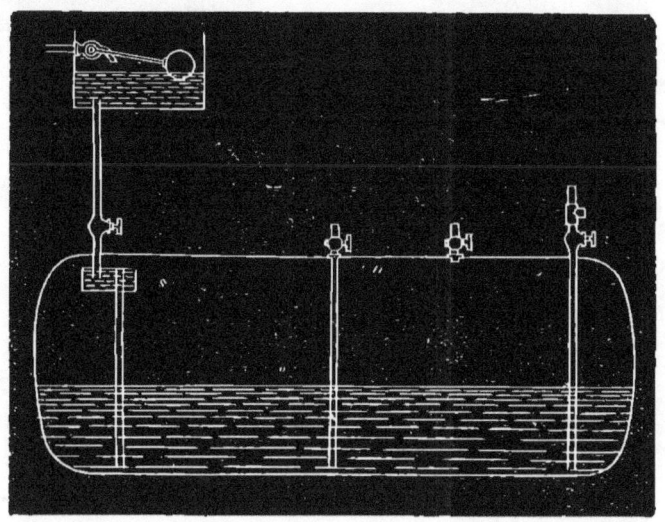

Fig. 20.

the cistern C, and the surface of the water in the cup inside the holder. No matter how much or how little gas be in the holder, the pressure is always uniform. The pressure can be increased or decreased by increasing or decreasing the distance between the two surfaces of the water, as before stated. G is the gas outlet, I is the inlet, W is the pipe to empty the holder when filling with gas. For a fixed apparatus, this one, perhaps, presents the best advantages.

4

Portable gas-holders have also had the careful consideration of scientific men, and at Fig. 21 will be seen an excellent form of

Fig. 21.

Fig. 22.

portable gas-holder, designed by Mr. S. Highley, which was exhibited by him in the Exhibition of 1862, and is described by him thus :—

"This I originally designed for a professor's lecture-room, where only small quantities of oxygen were required at a time, for the display of an occasional diagram in illustrating a course of lectures, and to avoid the daily and frequent production of oxygen. Fig. 22 shows how I contrived this arrangement, so that the lantern could be packed in the body of the gasometer for travelling, if necessary."

When unpacked and arranged as in Fig. 21, it will be seen that the "bell" which holds the gas is square, instead of cylindrical,

Fig. 24.

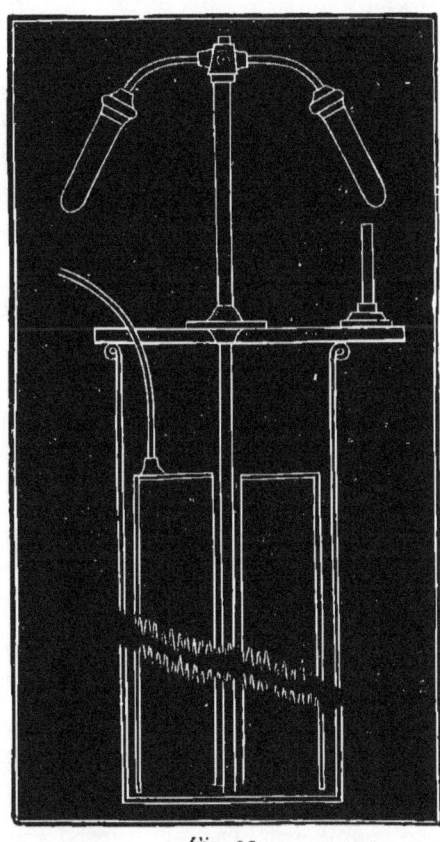

Fig. 23.

and slides into a double casing, shown in section (Fig. 22), that is filled with water, so as to form an air-tight water-joint for the run of the bell, and to reduce the bulk of the water required to a minimum. It was also designed as a stand for the lantern as shown. Although this apparatus was well adapted for the lecturer, experimentalist, or photographer, it was of insufficient capacity for lantern exhibitors generally. The want of some apparatus by which a supply of oxygen could be maintained

4—2

in connection with a portable gas-holder was in 1868 supplied by Mr. M. Noton, who was the first to describe the generating of oxygen gas at the time of consumption, by means of small retorts charged with plugs of chlorate of potash and oxide of manganese, which were alternately subjected to the flame of a Bunsen burner, thus generating the gas as occasion required, which was stored in the small portable gas-holder forming a part of the apparatus, and used therefrom (see Fig. 23). The plugs used were moulded while the mixture was in a damp state, and, after being dried, were ready for use.

A difficulty was experienced in extracting the spent plugs for re-charging, which necessitated the use of four, six, or more retorts, depending upon the quantity of gas required.

To obviate this difficulty, and to dispense with a number of retorts, the author designed a retort in which flat cakes could be used instead of plugs or cylinders. It was also arranged with due consideration to perfect safety, and the entire removal of fear from the minds of inexperienced experimentalists.

The principle of the retort or generator will be clearly seen from the accompanying woodcut (Fig. 24). It consists of two pieces, a flat plate, and a bell-shaped cap, supported by a stand in which is placed a Bunsen burner of improved construction. The cap has an aperture at the top, in which is screwed a pipe, etc., for conveying away the oxygen as made. In other respects the retort proper consists of two simple iron castings turned and ground to a gas-tight fit. The fastening consists of a bow, clearly shown in the woodcut, at the extremities of which are small spiral springs, so adjusted as to maintain a pressure equal to 1½ lbs. per square inch, which pressure is far in excess of what is ordinarily required for lime light purposes. Now, it is obvious, should the passage from the retort be closed (although in this apparatus there

is no likelihood of such an occurrence), the pressure in the retort
would rise until it had arrived at a pressure of 1½ lbs. per square
inch, when the gas would escape through the joint; and, as soon
as the passage was clear again, the gas would take its right course,
relieving the pressure inside the retort, and by virtue of the spring
the joint would close, and the top assume its original position.
When exhibiting this apparatus at several scientific societies, to
illustrate its safety qualities, as the gas was coming off rapidly the
outlet pipe was closed (by means of a tap purposely introduced),

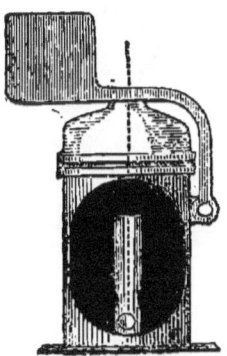

Fig. 25.   Fig 26.

and the oxygen, still being generated, escaped through the joint
(as intended) with perfect safety. To open the retort for re-charging,
etc., pull over the wood handle fixed to the top of the bow, and
the cap may be then removed by the wood handle fixed thereto,
and, to close the apparatus, reverse these operations. The handles
being made of wood prevent the fingers from being burned when
in use.

The method of making the cakes is as follows : To four parts
chlorate of potash and one part manganese, add sufficient water
to moisten, not to wet; after mixing well, fill the mould, using
little pressure, smooth off the surplus with a dinner knife or a

spatula, turn over, and the cakes will leave the mould entire. After sufficient cakes are thus made, they are set to dry, either by gentle heat or spontaneously; when dry, the bottoms are coated by dipping into a mixture of manganese and water about the consistency of cream; when dry, they are ready for use. This coating of the bottom of the cakes with plain manganese is to prevent the spent cake sticking to the retort, being the only part in contact with it. These cakes leave the retort in their entirety, only

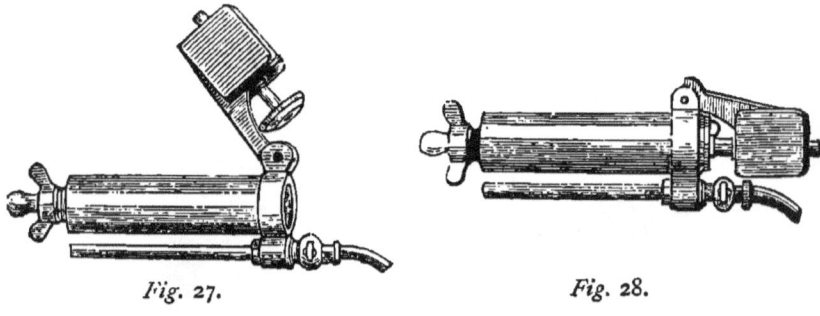

Fig. 27.   *Fig.* 28.

somewhat distended; they are easy to produce, clean to handle, and as hard as a piece of coal.

In addition to the retort shown at Fig. 24, other forms were devised by the writer.

The one, Fig. 25, for dead weight. Another, Fig. 26, for lever and weight.

The writer has also designed a retort for the use of plugs or cylinders, to which was applied the safety-valve in the dead-weight form. The principle will be fully understood by reference to the drawings; Fig. 27 showing the retort open; Fig. 28 showing it closed. If the pressure in the retort should from any cause rise in excess of that to which it is weighted, the gas would be liberated at the front end by virtue of the weight which is hinged to the

retort, and has attached to it the cap-lid in such a manner as not
to be quite rigid, but is free to move a little so as to find its proper position.   On the cap-lid is a small projection shown in Fig.
28, for the purpose of removing any substance which might interfere with the joint, and also permits of the lid being ground into
its proper bed.   The method of opening and closing the retort is

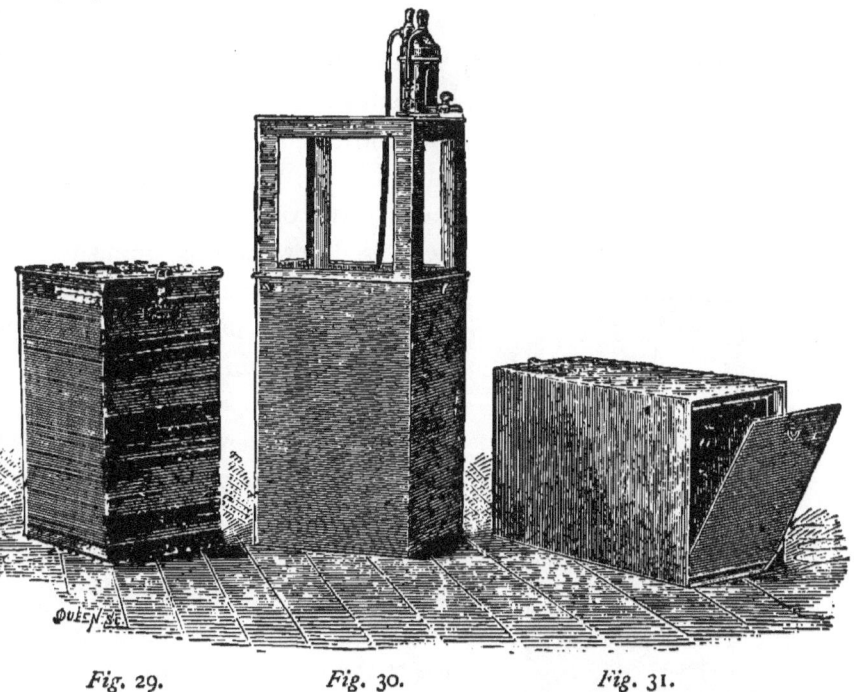

Fig. 29.   Fig. 30.   Fig. 31.

simple :—Turn up the weight and the retort is open, or turn down
the weight and it is closed.   Plugs of chlorate of potash and manganese may be made and used in thin sheet-iron cases, if preferred; or another method adopted is to make the plugs on a
wire, with a sheet-iron disc at the bottom end, and a small loop at
the other (just resembling a sugar-crusher).

As soon as the plugs are dry (which they become much sooner than when bottled up in a tin case), dip them in plain manganese and water; this, when dry, prevents any adhering to the retort. Should the plug break, or any part become detached, the disc at the plug end attached to the wire, on being extracted, brings all with it.

At Fig. 29 the whole apparatus is shown packed for travelling, with lanterns, &c., in a dry compartment. Fig. 30 shows the apparatus as at work. Fig. 31 shows the under side of the apparatus; and the lid, with lock-up arrangement, partly open, displays the portion used for packing, formed by the displacement-chamber, around which the water luting for the bell is poured when in action. Fig. 32 illustrates the apparatus used as a stand for the lantern.

Fig. 32.

When in use the pressure is applied by placing water in a reservoir provided for that purpose, thereby maintaining one uniform pressure throughout, which can be regulated according to the quantity of water used. If more convenient, any other substance than water may be adopted for weighting.

Thus by using this apparatus, portability is obtained, gas-bags, pressure boards, and weights are dispensed with, and a continuous supply of oxygen of even pressure with perfect safety is maintained.

CONDENSED GASES.

In America, where oxygen is manufactured commercially, cylinders of sheet iron (Fig. 33) were introduced, into which both oxygen and hydrogen were compressed to about 250 lbs. or 300 lbs. per square inch. This plan was also adopted in Brussels, where oxygen is largely used for ordinary illuminating purposes. It has also been introduced into this country, and is now sold commercially at so much per cubic foot, and, although possessing the excellent advantages of portability and convenience, in many ways it is nevertheless open to objection and serious drawbacks, as the apparatus for filling the cylinders is too costly for most amateurs. It is necessary to send them to the manufacturer to be refilled; this is in itself an expense, and in many cases a loss of time. But the most serious objection is that the cylinders often prove to be empty when they are expected to be full, through some leaky joint or connection, unless they are very well made, owing to the high pressure used, which is ever varying—another serious defect in the system. It will be clearly seen that, whatever pressure be used at the commencement, after half the gas is consumed, the remaining half must

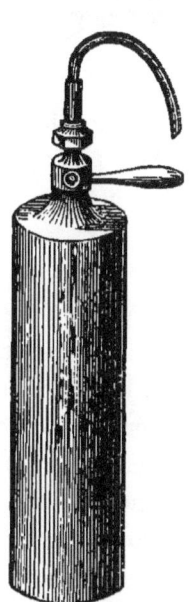

Fig. 33.

have expanded to double the volume, and therefore only half the original pressure remains, and so it goes on continually decreasing in pressure, and requiring constant attention at the jets or tap provided for the purpose. To obviate this constant attention, several forms of automatic valves and regulators have from time to time been introduced, but up to the present none of any practical use are before the public in a reliable form. We have heard much of the use our American friends make of condensed gas cylinders, and in reply the author would say that he has witnessed many exhibitions in the United States, conducted by the best lanternists of America, and, in every case where cylinders were used, only a single lantern was in operation, and generally their lantern manipulation was not first-class, or, at all events, not such as would satisfy many English lanternists we could name.

THE ETHOXO LIME LIGHT.

Before leaving the sources of illumination, the "Ethoxo" Lime Light must not be omitted. Undoubtedly the credit for the introduction of this light is due to Mr. William Broughton, and may be described briefly by stating that ether ($C_4 H_5 O$) is used in place of hydrogen. Various forms of vapourizers have been introduced, but that by Mr. Broughton is, in the writer's experience, decidedly the best.

The illumination is quite equal to most forms of oxy-hydrogen when blow-through jets are used, providing a good pressure be sustained. But there is a certain danger attending it that precludes the writer from recommending it (in its present form, at all events), except by those who thoroughly understand the nature of the substances in use. The author feels that in writing a book of this class, which may fall into the hands of many whose experience in such matters is very limited, that it becomes his duty to caution such persons from using something that might endanger life. At the same time, it would be manifestly unjust to Mr. Broughton not to refer to this light.

After reviewing the various sources of illumination, the modes of preparation and storing the gases, the author is brought to the conclusion that for really first-class exhibitions, where the *very best* results are desired, and which have to be conducted in various parts of the town or country, there is no better arrangement up to the present time, everything considered, than a pair of gas-bags, and double-pressure frame, using mixed jets.

JETS.

By far the most powerful and economical form of jet is the Oxy-hydrogen (Fig. 34) often called the Mixed Jet. As will be seen in the illustration, each gas is carried in a separate tube to a chamber under the nozzle, in which chamber the gases are mixed

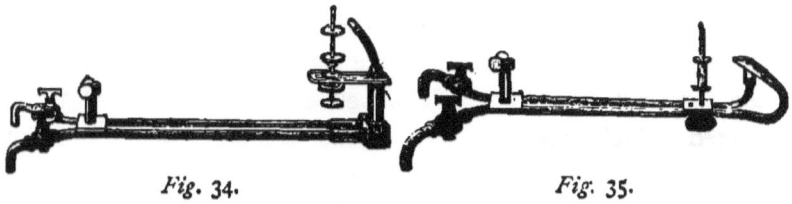

Fig. 34.   *Fig.* 35.

just before ignition. For the successful working of this jet it is imperative that both the oxygen and hydrogen be under equal pressure (see description of Double Pressure Frame, p. 40).

Originally the oxygen and hydrogen were mixed in the bag, in the proportion of one part by volume of oxygen to two of hydrogen, and only one tube was necessary; but this was a most dangerous proceeding, for should the pressure be relieved by any chance from the bag containing the mixed gases at the time the light was burning at the nozzle of the jet, the combustion would be instantly carried down the supply-tube and a fearful explosion would ensue. It was found safer therefore, to use the gases in separate bags, and to mix them in the chamber for that purpose just previous to ignition at the nozzle of the jet; but even in this case, if the bags be not equally weighted (a case which might easily occur through unequal sizes of bags or pressure boards, or by substituting manual pressure for weights), the gas under the heaviest pressure would be forced into the other bag, and, as in the former case, the relieving of the pressure would terminate the proceedings with equally dangerous results.

An accident of this class occurred in the presence of the writer, through a gentleman inadvertently putting his foot on to the bag to give a little more pressure : as soon as he withdrew it a fearful crash was heard; fortunately no one was injured, but the sudden concussion of the air produced a temporary deafness, besides more or less destruction to all the apparatus around.

So let it be borne in mind that when using mixed gases, never to relieve the pressure or adjust the bags or weights in any case when the light is burning. The best effect from a mixed jet is obtained at high pressures. The author has used this form of jet at a pressure equal to a column of water 120 inches in height : in this instance it is necessary to use hard limes, and a clockwork arrangement to automatically rotate the limes, and gradually give them an upward spiral motion.

"*The safety*" oxy-hydrogen, or "*blow-through*" jet, although inferior in illuminating power to the above, is usually sufficient for pictures of 12 to 14 feet diameter; but it must be mentioned that more gas is consumed to produce the same result than is required with the mixed gases. With this jet it is only necessary that the oxygen be under pressure, the hydrogen may be used direct from the main ; this is a great convenience in many instances. It will be seen in Fig. 35 that in this jet the gases are mixed at the nozzle, and therefore all fear of a catastrophe through the gases becoming mixed, even under unequal pressure, is abolished.

The hydrogen is conducted up the left-hand tube, the extremity or nozzle of which is of wide bore, the oxygen being conveyed in the right-hand tube, and from a fine nozzle is blown through the hydrogen. Softer limes may be used with this jet to advantage.

The effect of the gas upon the lime is to puncture it, causing small cavities; and when a cavity has been formed, the light is by no means so effective, and there is a great liability of the flame being thrown forward, thereby endangering the condenser by fracture. It is necessary, therefore, to slightly rotate the lime after showing each picture, and this is most conveniently done after dissolving, and when the light is turned low.

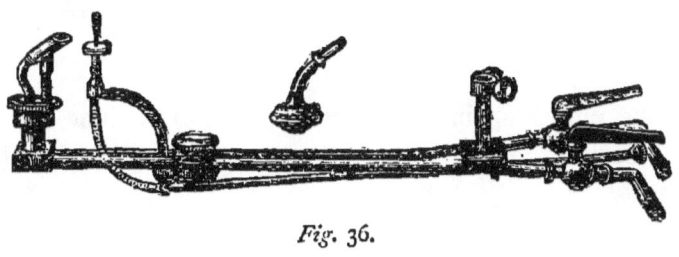

Fig. 36.

Several means for rotating the limes have been devised to work from the rear of the lantern. An exceedingly ingenious arrange ment was some time ago introduced, which will be seen at Fig. 36, consisting of a spiral spring connecting the vertical lime pin, with the long horizontal rod, on the end of which is a milled head, a little beyond the taps of the jets.

This jet forms a blow-through, and a high pressure or mixed jet, by simply unscrewing a collar and substituting one nozzle for another.

In the jet, illustrated at Fig. 37, brass cog-wheels are used in connection with a screwed lime pin to range and turn the lime, and although slightly more expensive than the foregoing jet, is a a far better arrangement. Mr. Place, optician, has introduced a very excellent form of jet, the lime pin being provided with a very quick pitch thread or screw, so that one turn of the pin raises the lime about an eighth of an inch, and so prevents

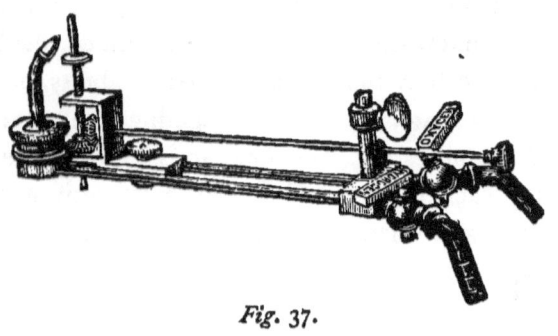

Fig. 37.

the flame projecting into the hole worn out in the lime, upon the completion of a revolution, as is the case with the very fine thread lime pins.

OXY-CALCIUM OR SPIRIT JET.

This jet is only used when hydrogen is not obtainable or inconvenient to get at. Many modifications of this style have been devised with more or less success. That illustrated at Fig. 38 is a good form.

It is very essential that the reservoir for the spirit of wine be kept cool, also accessible

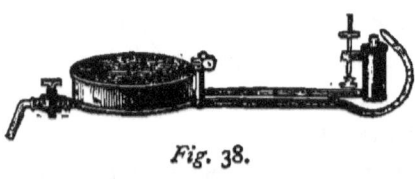

Fig. 38.

for recharging with spirit, and that the wick-holder be made to hold a large wick capable of giving a good compact flame.

No possible chance of explosion could occur with this form of jet, though the writer has known of clumsy operators setting fire to the spirits.

Soft limes should be used with it, and large nozzles, with not too excessive a pressure, have been found to produce the best results.

The taps of oxy-hydrogen jets should be lacquered of different colours, so as to be distinguishable in the dark.

Fig 39.

It is important that no solder be used in the construction of the jets, and that the nozzles are removable or accessible for cleaning. In jets of the best quality the nozzles are made of platinum. The lime-pins should be large enough to hold two limes one above the other, so that in case of accident to one lime another is close at hand, warm and ready for use. A small pair of tongs are useful in removing broken limes.

A most ingenious burner has been devised for use with the Sciopticon, by Mr. L. Marcy, the inventor of that instrument. It takes the exact position of the oil lamp. This burner is provided with three separate nozzles, and can be used as a mixed gas-jet, a blow-through jet, or for oxy-calcium lime light. It is shown at Fig. 39. The body D is formed of a block of hard wood, upon which the various parts are mounted. At O and H are the taps for

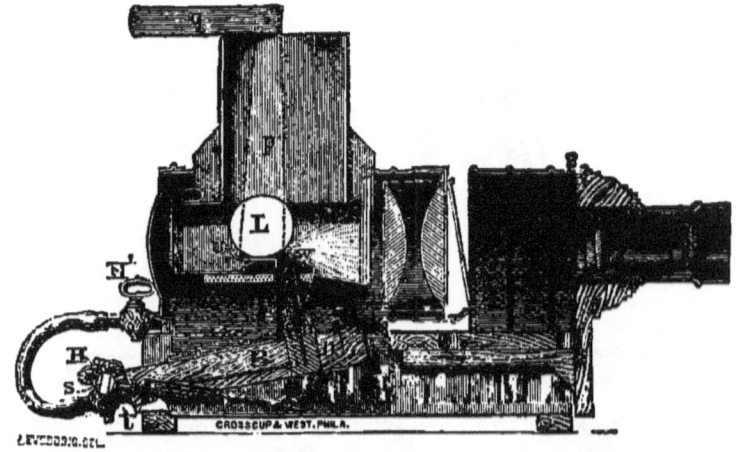

Fig. 40.

the admission of oxygen and hydrogen, and which are made dissimilar, so that each may be readily distinguished in the dark. Between these taps is a screw with a milled head at s for raising or lowering the jet to the required position. The lime L, which is of disc form, is so placed that the flame impinges upon its circumference, and therefore a great amount of surface is available. The lime-holder is placed through the chimney aperture, and is held in position by the piece attached at right angles, as shown in the illustration.

The lime is easily turned in its cradle. At D and E are two boxes in which the two jets not in use are kept, and F is a brass door for closing same. At V is a small piece of steel, mounted with brass milled head, which can be used to clean the jets when required. The whole is very accessible for cleaning, and capable of every adjustment. It is shown in position at Fig. 40.

The three different jets are illustrated at Figs. 41, 42, 43.

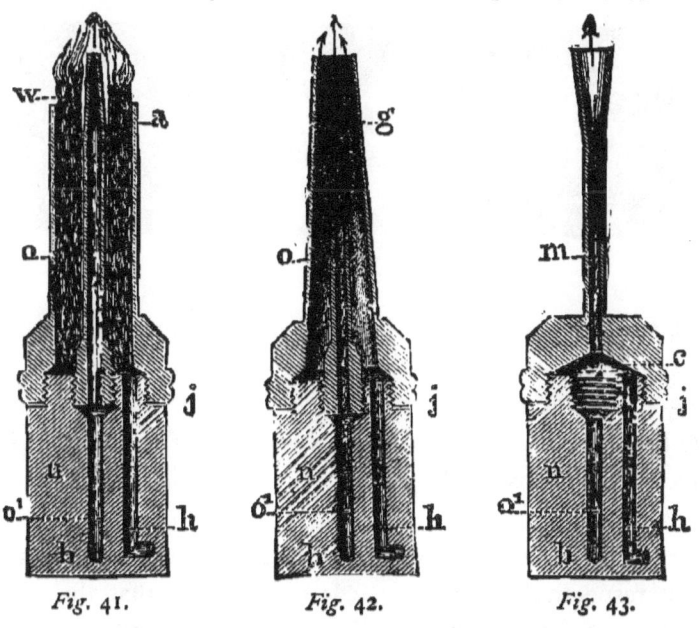

Fig. 41.   *Fig.* 42.   *Fig.* 43.

Fig. 41 represents the one used for the alcohol flame or oxycalcium jet; the wick w being fed through the hydrogen-tap from a reservoir of alcohol, with which each burner is supplied.

Fig. 42 represents the blow-through jet, and Fig. 43 the oxyhydrogen or mixed jet, each gas being conveyed through its respective tube O or H, and is mixed in the small chamber at C previous to emerging through the nozzle M.

5

As before stated, it is only by the use of mixed gases that an explosion can occur, for both oxygen and hydrogen are perfectly harmless if kept to themselves, as hydrogen will not burn unless oxygen be present, and though oxygen is the supporter of combustion, it will not burn alone; therefore it is clear that so long as these gases are kept separate no danger can accrue.

To provide against the possibility of accident when using mixed

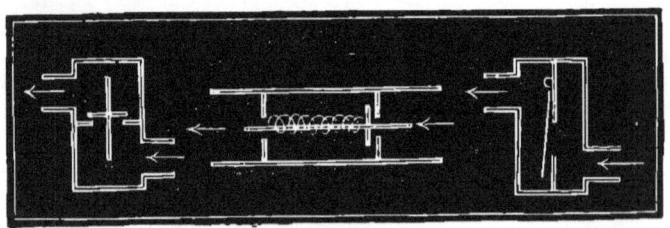

Fig. 44.

gases, various devices have been proposed, some very ingenious, and some very inefficient, with the object of preventing the flame being drawn down the supply-pipes. Layers of fine wire gauze have been introduced into the supply-tubes. This plan was found inefficient, as an oxy-hydrogen flame could easily be made to pass through the gauze.

Mr. J. T. Taylor devised three different forms of safety valves, shown respectively at Fig. 44. It will be seen that the two outside ones are only intended to be used in the positions shown in the woodcut. The centre one is by far the best arrangement, and possesses the advantage of being used in any position, therefore it is the most approved form. It consists of a metal valve, and a fine spiral spring, so adjusted that very little force is required to open it, and remaining closed in its normal position prevents any return of gas.

Gurney's arrangement was to pass the gas through a slight

column of water under the jet; but this was not a convenient arrangement, and in many cases was not effective.

Mr. S. Highley improved upon this latter plan by an additional valve, and with his arrangement an explosion would be impossible. But even this plan was not without fault, being somewhat complicated, and the writer has often known lanternists to shirk the use of many good things on account of the extra trouble in their adoption. He has therefore devised a valve styled a "back-pressure valve," clearly illustrated at Fig. 45. It consists of two parts made in brass, between which is placed a thin india-rubber or oiled silk diaphragm, through which four or five holes are made, as shown at B. The area of these orifices is in excess of the ingress-tube, therefore the slightest pressure entering the valve in the direction of the arrow would act

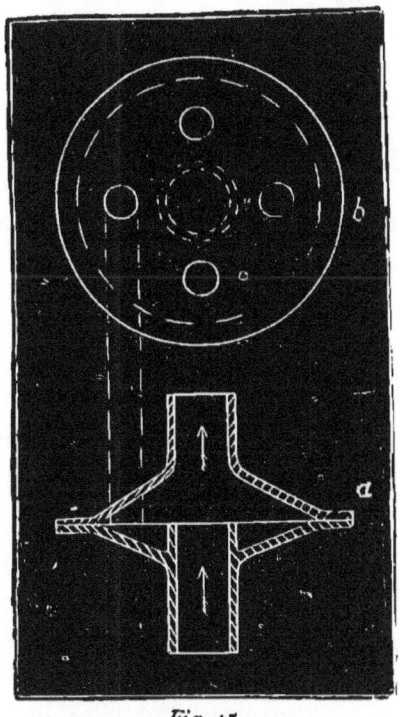

Fig. 45.

upon the diaphragm so as to open the valve, and allow the gas to pass with the least possible resistance on account of the large area of diaphragm exposed to pressure.

As the valve in its normal condition is closed, nothing whatever could pass the opposite way, and the greater the pressure in this direction the tighter would the valve be closed. Both india-rubber and oiled silk withstand the action of the gases moderately well; but should occasion ever require, the valve could be readily taken to pieces, and a new diaphragm be inserted in a few minutes. This valve has been subjected to most severe tests, and in no one instance has it failed to act efficiently. A moment's reflection will show that no such appliances are at all necessary when using blow-through jets, but, in the case of mixed jets, a back-pressure valve should be used on each supply pipe, placed as near the lantern as possible.

A short time ago Mr. Broughton introduced a flame interceptor, consisting of a small chamber, which was filled with powdered pumice and fixed under the nozzle of the jet. This has been considered very effectual in performing its functions.

PHOTOMETRY.

IN estimating or measuring light, instruments are necessary, called Photometers, the standard of comparison being a candle, defined by Act of Parliament as a sperm candle of six to the pound, and burning at the rate of 120 grains per hour, and, although such candles are offered for sale, it seems unfortunate that no better standard was fixed upon, as candles, commercially, are not manufactured alike in different places, and the varying quality of the material, together with the thickness of the wicks, make serious differences in the results of experiments in consequence.

We hope, ere long, to see a better and universal standard accepted by all nations, as several have already been brought to notice, and others are still being submitted.

Of the various forms of " Photometers," the simplest are, perhaps, the "Rumford" or the "Bunsen." At Fig. 46 is an illustration of the former, the principle being based upon the comparison of shadows. The light to be tested should be placed at some given distance from the screen, which may be transparent and viewed from behind, or opaque and viewed in front. A rod is then fixed a few inches from the screen, on which a shadow will be thrown.

Fig. 46.

. Now place the candle at such a distance that another shadow of equal depth is seen alongside the first one. The distance of each should be measured off, each measurement should be squared, and on dividing the greater by the lesser, the quotient will be the illuminating candle power.

"Bunsen's Photometer" consists of a white paper screen, with a grease-spot in the centre. The light to be tested is placed at a given distance on one side of the screen, and the candle at the other, the distance being regulated so that the grease-spot appears neither lighter nor darker than the rest of the screen—in fact, is invisible from either side. The respective distances are now measured off, and their squares are proportional to the illuminating powers. In comparing lights no optical arrangements should be used, as this would seriously interfere with the results. Thus, in testing the lime light, the jet should be entirely removed from the lantern, and tested without being shown through either condenser or objective.

A series of experiments were gone into by the author, in which both "Rumford's" and "Bunsen's" Photometers were used, both kinds being adopted, so as to check the results. Below will be found the averages of several illuminating powers, as resulting from those experiments:—

Sciopticon	41.7	standard candles.
Oxy-calcium	152	,, ,,
Safety or blow-through jet .	208	,, ,,
Oxy-hydrogen or mixed gases	430	,, ,,

DISSOLVING VIEWS.

DISSOLVING VIEWS were originally invented by Mr. Henry Langdon Childe, who in 1811 publicly exhibited them for the first time. The effect was produced, as now, by the employment of two lanterns, with an apparatus arranged in front of the objective lenses, whereby the light from one lantern is admitted on the screen at the same time that the light from the other is obliterated. This apparatus is styled the "Dissolver," and at Fig. 47 will be seen a pair of lanterns with the same applied. It consists of a serrated plate or comb, placed in front óf the objectives, and attached to a vertical bar with a rackwork and pinion; a handle at the back of the lanterns, so placed as to be accessible to the operator, gives motion to the rack and pinion, which moves the comb vertically, thereby alternately shutting out

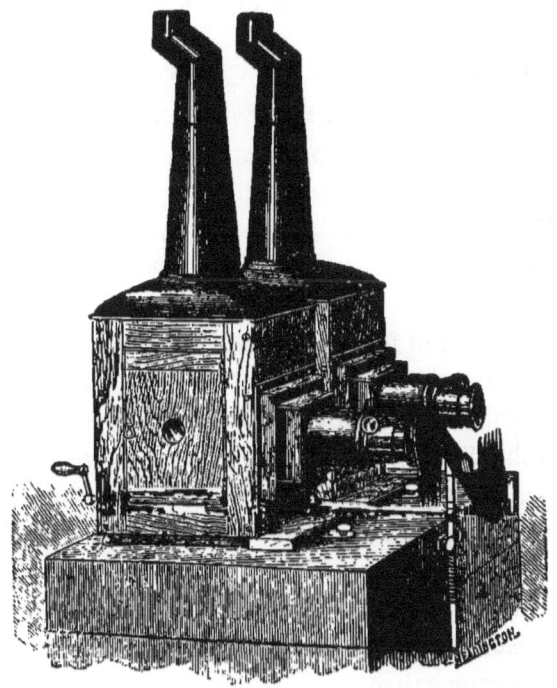

Fig. 47.

the light from each lantern. In the illustration the right-hand lantern is closed, while the left-hand one is full open, and a picture in this lantern is supposed to be projected on the screen. Now, by turning the handle, the "Dissolver" will rise, and in so doing will gradually open the right-hand lantern objective; at the same time it will as gradually cover that of the left-hand lantern:

thus one picture is caused to fade away at the same time that another one is made to appear.

The blending into each other of the pictures (with no increase or decrease of illumination) is such that the transformation, when suitable pictures are selected, is most wonderfully beautiful and fairylike.

Prior to the introduction of Mr. Childe's Dissolving Views, the lantern was considered merely as a toy, and not of educational value.

Probably the earliest employment of the Magic Lantern to educational purposes was originated by the late Mr. Richard Vaughan Yates, of Liverpool. Mr. Yates, having made a tour in the Holy Land, on his return had a number of paintings on glass, executed by some of the best artists of the day, to illustrate the principal places of interest visited during his travels.

Mr. Yates, assisted by Mr. Dancer, optician, at that time of Liverpool, exhibited these views to delighted audiences. The late Mr. John Smith, one of the proprietors of the *Liverpool Mercury*, was so impressed by these exhibitions, as showing the lantern's importance as an educational instrument, that he arranged an extended course of lectures on geography, to be illustrated by aid of the lantern. These lectures were delivered and illustrated by the above means in all the principal towns of the kingdom, and proved very remunerative.

The illumination of lantern exhibitions up to this period had been effected by means of oil lamps, which did not prove satisfactory in some of the larger rooms, and in 1837, Mr. Dancer, optician, then of Manchester, suggested to Mr. Smith the use of the "lime light," or, as it was then styled, the "Drummond light," which at that time was in use for gas microscopes only.

The artists who painted the slides predicted that their pictures would be ruined by such a light.

The new illuminating power supplied Mr. Smith's wants admirably, and the success of these lectures at once induced Mr. James Robinson, of Liverpool, to commence in a similar line, and Mr. Dancer supplied him with an elaborate oxy-hydrogen lantern, having 9-inch condensers. The directors of the Manchester Mechanics' Institution have largely contributed to popularize the Magic Lantern as an educational instrument, and their annual exhibition proved very remunerative and attractive. To Mr. Dancer is due the credit also of having first exhibited photographs in the lantern, the first one being of the programme at the above institution. At this time Messrs. Negretti & Zambra were the sole agents for the magnificent stereoscopic slides of M. Ferrier, of Paris, and a number of these slides were sent down by them to Manchester. Mr. Dancer prepared them for the lantern by dissolving away the white wax with which they were backed, and under the excellent management of Mr. E. Hutchins, the Secretary of the above institution, these exhibitions justly obtained a wide celebrity, and many other public institutions throughout the kingdom were prompted to enter into a similar enterprise with more or less success.

Now that the introduction of photography in connection with the Magic Lantern had become instituted, its value as an educational instrument became more apparent, for although many of the hand-painted slides were very beautiful and artistically produced, a single picture costing in some instances as much as twenty guineas, yet the artist, however eminent, can never aspire to the accuracy of photography in minute detail.

A climax would now seem to have been reached when Mr. Dancer conceived the idea of dissolving by shutting off the gas from one lantern and, at the same time, turning it on to the other lantern. For this purpose he had taps arranged to shut off the gases from each lantern alternately, thereby dispensing with the

mechanical dissolver already described.   The first of these was
made by Mr. Dancer for the Manchester Mechanics' Institution,
which, on being tried, surpassed in result all expectation, for not
only was the dissolving better, but about 50 per cent. of the gas
was saved.

Mr. Noton afterwards devised a Single Plug Dissolver, and published a description of it in the *British Journal of Photography*,
March 15th, 1864.

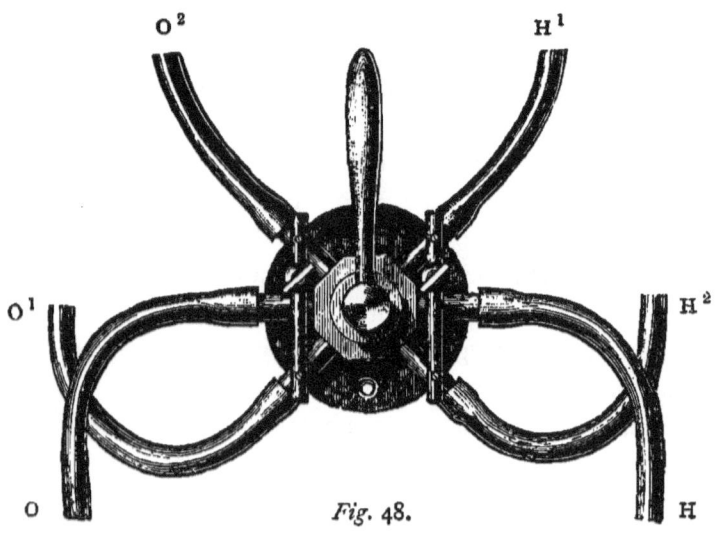

Fig. 48.

It has proved equally applicable with the mixed jet, the safety
blow-through, and the oxy-calcium lime light, and has, since its
introduction, been modified in various ways, with pretty much the
same result.

The Universal Gas Dissolver, shown at Fig. 48, is a modification
of the Single Plug Dissolver, shewn by Mr. Noton.   As will be
seen, this tap consists of a single plug, in which two cavities are
cut in such positions that the gases enter at their respective

branches indicated by o and H, and when the lever is upright the passage is clear to both lanterns.

o^1 and H^1 must be connected to the jet of one lantern, and o^2 and H^2 to the other. When the lever is drawn to the right hand, the gas is shut off from the top jet, and when to the left the bottom jet, enough gas escaping along the bye-passes, when the stop-cock is slightly open to keep the jet alight without shewing an image on the screen.

These small stop-cocks can be adjusted at the commencement of an exhibition to the size of light required. It is in many cases advantageous to have both lanterns fully illuminated at the same time for the production of effects, such as lightning, the bursting of shells, etc. This tap altogether is exceedingly well finished, and very accessible for cleaning.

Another very effective and simple dissolving tap is styled the "Polytechnic Gas-Dissolver," an illustration of which is at Fig. 49,

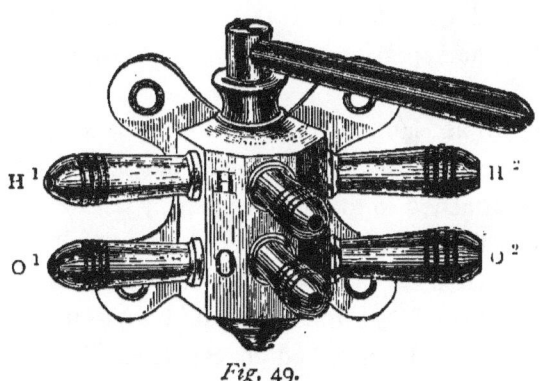

Fig. 49.

and consists of a single plug, arranged to cut off the gas from each lantern alternately; which, beside possessing the advantage of being able to have both lanterns fully illuminated at one time, by simply turning the lever to the back, both gases are shut off, as is sometimes required when a break or interval occurs in the entertainment for the introduction of, say, a little music. Thus the trouble of turning off the gas at the bags is avoided, and at restarting no adjustments are necessary. Provision is made in the plug so that the hydrogen may pass, so as to retain a faint light alternately in each lantern as the gases are shut off. In making the connections with this dissolver, the gases are to be introduced at the branches indicated, o and H, and the branches marked o^1 and H^1 must be connected with the jets of one lantern, and those marked o^2 and H^2 must be connected with the jets of the other.

The dissolving taps already described apply to the double or Biunial lantern, and for such are all that can be desired; but for a triple lantern it will be seen that some further arrangement will be necessary, and to this subject the writer has given considerable attention. Single plug dissolvers for triple lanterns have been made, and recommended as the most perfect and simple dissolver; but the experience of the writer does not bear this out in fact.

There are triple lanterns arranged with a six-way dissolver, Fig. 48, connected with the two lower jets, and a single or four-way dissolver attached to the top jet; but by far the most effective arrangement is that which the writer has successfully adopted for many years—that of a single or four-way dissolver to each jet. Recently Mr. Steward has made an addition to this system, consisting of vertical rods, attached to the levers by clamp tubes, thereby enabling any two, or all three, jets to be brought into combination, or use singly in an instant. These dissolvers are shown in positions at Fig. 55, page 78.

Dissolving taps and jets, however well made, require cleaning periodically, and before use they should be taken to pieces and cleaned. The pipes should be blown through to see that they are perfectly free and clean, and the nozzles of the jets should be cleaned with a piece of soft copper wire, and freed from any particles of lime which may have collected there. Plugs of the dissolvers and jets should be smeared with a trace of fine olive oil, and gas-bag taps are better lubricated with a little pure tallow. Burnt india-rubber has been recommended as a lubricant for the plugs of such apparatus as come in contact with oxygen, but this seems merely to be an excuse for a badly-fitting plug.

THE BIUNIAL LANTERN.

THIS lantern, illustrated at Fig. 50, combines two lanterns in one body, having their optical systems placed one above the other, and is the most popular form of dissolving view apparatus in general use.

The bodies are generally constructed of mahogany, which should be well seasoned, and provided with a sheet-iron lining, between which and the body there should be a cavity forming an air passage. The cavity should be open at the bottom, and the sheet-iron lining is generally made about a quarter of an inch higher than the body, so that the dome top does not rest on the wood body, but on the iron lining; thereby the air passage is open at the top also, and, forming a free passage for air, the lantern is kept cool. Two doors, one for each jet, are better than one large one, and in the best lanterns two doors are provided at each side, with blue glass windows fitted in brass cells, through which the light may be viewed when making adjustments, etc. The fronts may be of wood and tin, or wholly of brass, which latter is the best, and generally more rigid. The tubes are generally telescopic

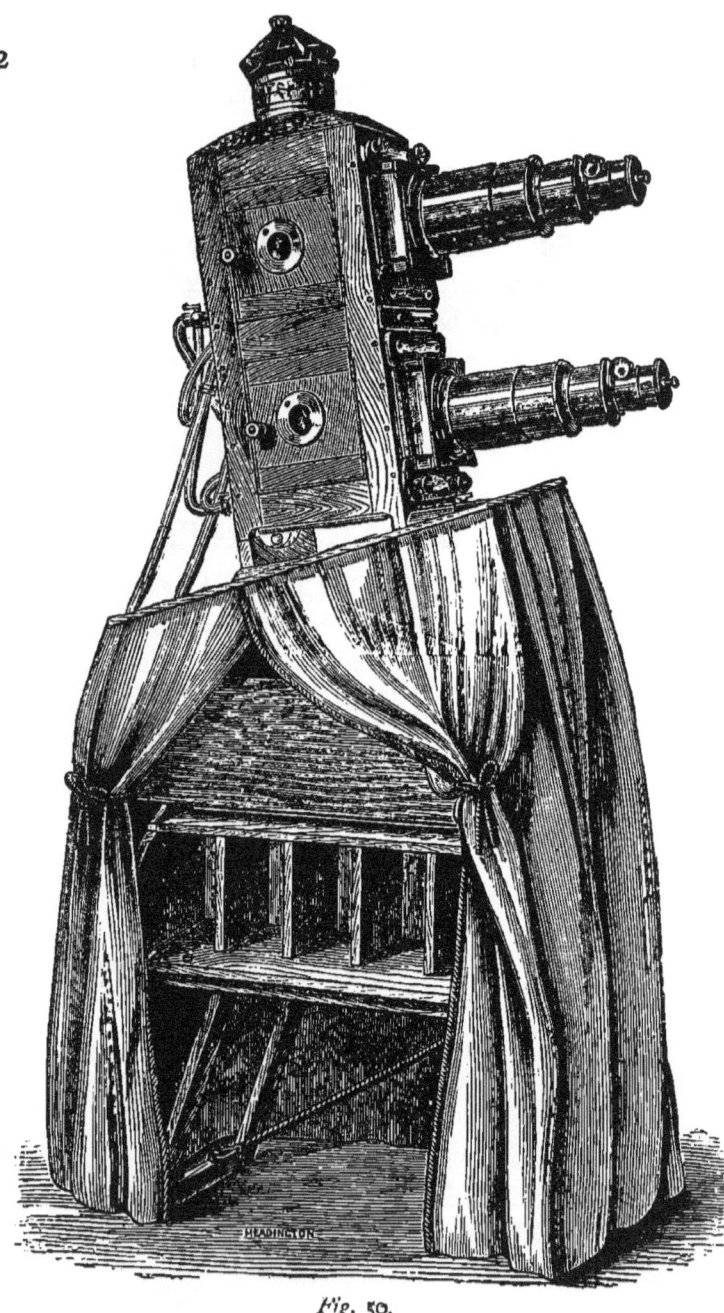

Fig. 50.

and provided with caps. The slide stage should be open top, bottom, and both sides, and provided with a roller curtain slide.

The discs are brought concentric on the screen by means of milled-headed screws in front, the lower optical system being hinged at the top, and the upper one hinged at the bottom, as shown in the illustration.

The jets and dissolving taps may be similar to those already described.

The packing box may be of any convenient form. Usually it is too low in itself to answer for a stand upon which to fix the lantern when in use. The illustration shows a box, in which slides and other accessories are packed, so constructed as to form a suitable stand, and, when covered with drapery of approved colour, and the lantern placed on the top, the whole forms a hand-some piece of apparatus.

THE "LUKE" BIUNIAL LANTERN.

THIS lantern is similar in construction to the Biunial previously described, except that the adjustment of the optical systems for centreing the discs is reversed, being hinged at the top and bottom, and the adjusting screws in the centre (see Fig. 51.) The body is constructed of stout japanned tin, which, though not so handsome in appearance, has the advantage of lightness, and for this reason is now used by many lecturers who are accustomed to travel about the country. The slide-stages are open top and bottom, as well as both sides, and provided with a

roller curtain shutter.   The condensers are 4 inches diameter and
the objectives achromatic, of long and short focus, with brass
sliding tubes.   The jets and dissolving tap may be equal to those

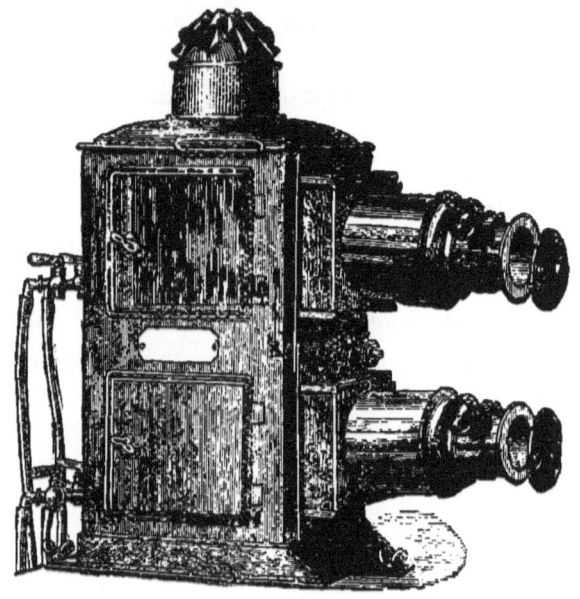

Fig. 51.

supplied with the very best lantern, and therefore the effect produced quite as good.   The packing case, which forms a stand,
measures 18 inches high, 17 inches wide, and 8½ inches deep.

DANCER'S LANTERN.

THIS lantern was one of the most perfect of its day. As will be seen (Fig. 52), one body combines in it the two optical systems, which are placed diagonally as shown. By this arrangement the centres are brought as near to each other as possible, still

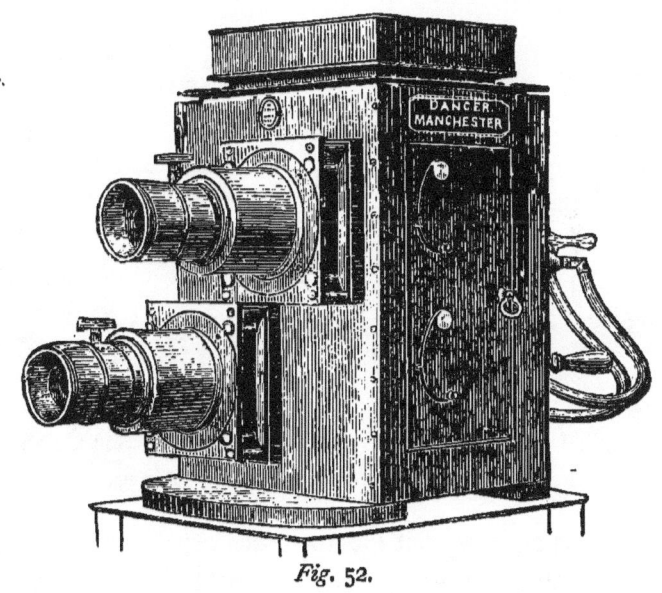

Fig. 52.

allowing ample room for the manipulation of the slides either horizontally or vertically, the latter being convenient for effects, such as balloon ascents, etc. The discs are brought concentric on the screen by an adjusting screw brought through and arranged at the back of the lantern. The heat emanating from the lower jet in no way affects the upper one; no tall chimney is requisite, and a neat flat top is arranged so that no light can escape, while ample provision is made for the exit of the heated air, and perfect ventilation is secured.

6

CHADWICK'S LANTERN.

I N the early part of the year 1878 the author introduced to the notice of the members of the Manchester Photographic Society a small pair of lanterns, which were admired for their neatness, simplicity, and compactness.   It will be seen in the illustra-

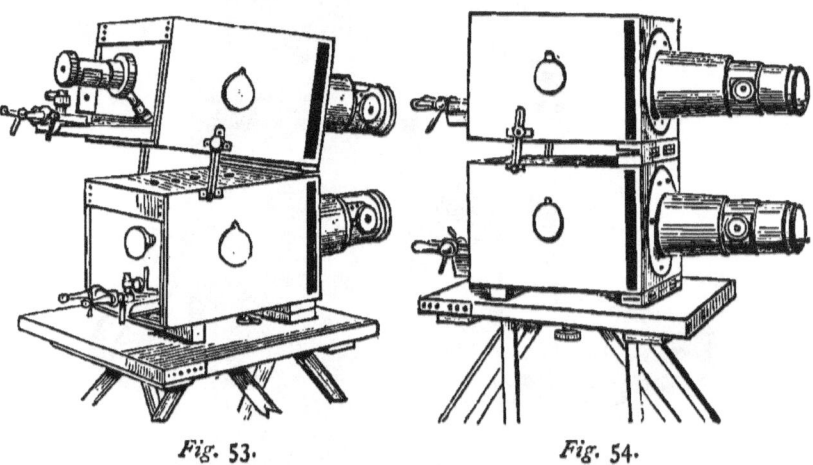

Fig. 53.   *Fig.* 54.

tions (Figs. 53 and 54) that the apparatus consists of two separate lanterns, placed one over the other. A hinged piece attached to the bottom of each lantern forms a means of coupling, and also allows of the adjustment necessary to bring the discs concentric on the screen.   When once adjusted, they are kept in position by two slotted bars and milled-headed screws, as shown in the illustrations.   The hinged piece on the bottom lantern also admits of any necessary adjustment, and also forms a means of securing the whole to a table, stand, or tripod top.   The bodies were made of mahogany, the inside dimensions being 5 inches square, lined with sheet tin (allowing an air space between the lining and the body), and so perforated as to prevent the emission of light, while securing perfect ventilation. The conical fronts holding the objectives were attached to the bodies by screws, the holes in the flanges of the fronts being slotted, so that they could be easily detached, and if required packed inside the lanterns. The apertures for the pictures were made of the standard width, in which were placed registering carriers, a description of which is given later. The jets may be of any approved form, and the lime and light can be viewed from the back by reflection from the condensers or through the blue glass windows in the sides. When necessary, a third lantern (an exact duplicate of the other two) can be placed on the top, or the two lanterns may be used side by side or singly. With these lanterns the author has shown large-size discs to the greatest perfection, and for an amateur who wishes to construct a lantern for his own use nothing can be much simpler.

THE TRIPLE LANTERN.

THIS elaborate instrument is in optical and mechanical detail similar to the Biunial, at page 72, with the addition of a third lantern placed on the top (Fig. 55), which may, however, be removed at will, and used as a single lantern. Also the two lower lanterns may be used as a complete biunial. The advantage of a third lantern for effects was no doubt first suggested by the Rev. Canon Beechey. Although many charming effects may be shown by a biunial lantern, they can generally be produced to better advantage by a triple lantern, and without going into the consideration of many elaborate examples of such slides and effects as can only be shown by a triple lantern, we will illustrate a simple instance with such an effect as nearly every lanternist will be acquainted; for instance, the Mosque of Omar. This usually consists of three slides: No. 1, the Mosque by daylight; No. 2, the Mosque by night; and No. 3, the effect to be used in conjunction

Fig. 55.

with No. 2 for illuminating the stained glass windows from within, and often in this slide the moon is made to appear. We will first see what can be done with these in a biunial lantern. No. 1 slide is shown by the first lantern; No. 2 slide with the second lantern. Next we will bring out the illumination of the windows with the first lantern, and to increase the effect of night we lower the light on No. 2; and if the moon is to be shown with No. 3, we produce a superior light upon it. Up to now the effect is splendid; but here comes in the difficulty. How are we to get the next subject on the screen, for we must remember both lanterns are engaged? Why, there is only one way, and that is to take away the light from the stained glass windows, and put out the moon, by raising the light on No. 2 slide to get away No. 3 for the next picture. Now, in the triple arrangement, we should leave the effect as it stood, and introduce the next subject in the third lantern, dissolving away Nos. 2 and 3 at the same time. For other illustrations see page 118. See also description of curtain roller slide for exhibiting statuary, page 121.

BEECHEY'S LANTERN.

UP to the present time dissolving views have been treated of as being produced by two or three lanterns, or with one lantern arranged with two or three separate lights. An idea for producing the above effect with one only, emanated from the Rev. Canon Beechey, who many years ago had a lantern constructed in which only one light was used to illuminate three distinct optical systems, and for the purpose of producing dissolving views and other dioramic effects. This lantern was first exhibited at the Exhibition of 1851, and is here illustrated at Fig. 56.

It consists, as shown in the diagram, of three separate optical systems emanating from one body, with prisms placed at the extremities of the side systems, which were placed at such angles that the discs from all three were concentric on the screen. The first illuminating power used was the oxy-hydrogen lime light, the cylinder form of lime being used, and which was supported upon a pin, this pin being fixed central with all three condensers. An unequal light was the result, the side systems receiving less than the centre one. As it was the inventor's intention not only to

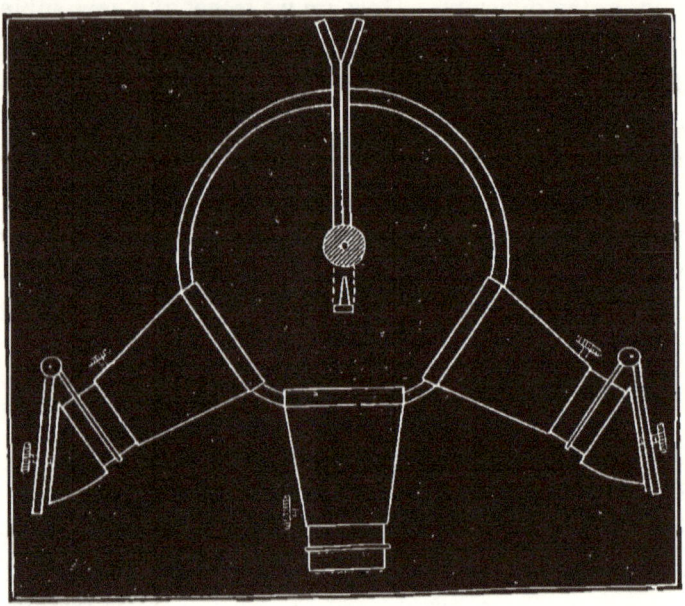

Fig. 56,

produce dissolving views, but also to have all three systems in operation at the same time when required for effects, &c., he therefore discarded the cylinder form of lime and substituted the spherical, which was suspended by a platinum wire over the flame of a fountain oil lamp, through the centre of which passed a gentle stream of oxygen. The whole of the lower portion of the lime was thus rendered luminously incandescent, and the rays of light collected by each system thus equalized. The oxygen nozzle being of large size, little pressure was needed, and therefore the lime was not so liable to split, as if a small nozzle and heavy pressures had been used. Although this oxy-calcium light was much inferior to oxy-hydrogen, it proved very successful for small-sized discs. A very perfect mechanical dissolver was attached, and the whole arrangement so simple and unique that we cannot but express surprise that the principle so long remained in *statu quo.*

This same idea of dissolving with one light has been adopted by M. Duboscq, of Paris, substituting the electric for the lime light. In Duboscq's apparatus, both sets or lenses were placed as close together as possible with convenience, and parallel to each other; a concave reflector being arranged to throw the light to each condenser alternately, while a very simple sliding dissolver opened and closed the objectives.

KEEVIL'S LANTERN.

ANOTHER form of dissolving lantern made its appearance a few years ago, based upon the original idea of Canon Beechey's (namely, dissolving with one light), and which was styled "Keevil's Patent Newtonian Lantern," illustrations of which are shown at Figs. 57 and 58. It is duplex in form, being fitted with one optical system, projecting in front, shown at A, and another projecting from one side, as shown at B. The light through the system A is transmitted on to the screen direct, in the usual way. At the extremity of the system B is fixed a prismatic lens, by which means a disc can be projected on to the screen, central with the one from A. The oxy-hydrogen jet is arranged on a pivot, which is a fixture in the bottom of the lantern, the centre of rotation being as near the outside surface of the lime cylinder as possible; and by rotating the burner through about a quarter of a circle, the light is brought central with each condenser alternately, and simul-

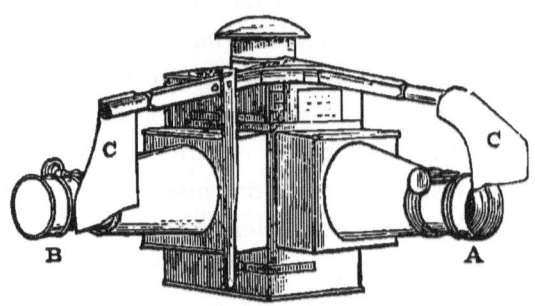

Fig. 57.

taneously the mechanical dissolver (c c) opens and closes the objectives. To compensate for any loss of light occasioned by the use of the prism, the condenser of this system is made somewhat shorter in focus than the other one, evenness of illumination being thereby secured. Both objectives are made achromatic, and the definition of the one to which the prism is attached is very little inferior to the ordinary one. The jets never require adjustment,

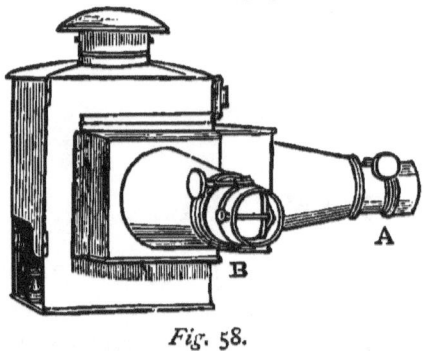

Fig. 58.

as each lantern is put to a practical test before being sent out; the best position for the jet being thereby obtained, further adjustment becomes unnecessary. The dissolving apparatus is adjustable and fairly efficient. The conical fronts are easily detached, and if required it can be used as a single lantern.

Its small dimensions are much in its favour, the whole packing into a small box, easily carried in the hand.

THE OPAQUE LANTERN.

MAGIC Lantern pictures are called Transparencies because they are shown by light transmitted through them; but a very wide range of opaque subjects can be exhibited upon the screen, and made highly interesting, by an instrument introduced first in a practical form by Messrs. Chadburn, in which photographs, cartes-de-visite, engravings, drawings, and other opaque objects, such as minerals, crystals, shells, plaster casts, medals, cameos, coins, small flowers, watches in motion, the human hand and face, and an infinite variety of subjects, may be exhibited with their natural colours and shades.

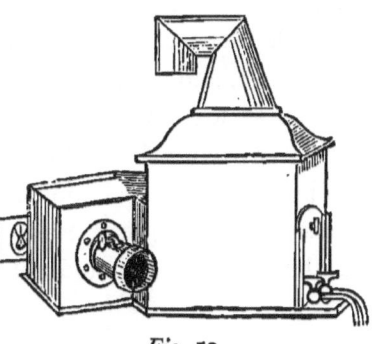

Fig. 59.

Its construction (see Fig. 59) consists of a lantern box, in which is fixed a pillar to which the lime-cylinder is attached, and behind it is a large silvered reflector, accessible for adjustment, which can be raised or lowered, moved backwards or forwards; the light it receives being thrown upon the condenser, and thereby concentrated upon the picture or object placed in the sliding door of the angular box which joins up to the square compartment. The illuminated picture or object is then received by the achromatic-objective, and projected upon the screen. The angular compartment can be detached and replaced with ordinary lantern fronts, and direct light with transparent pictures can be used. The half of an orange, if squeezed and placed in this lantern, has a particularly grotesque effect.

A convenient adaptation to the ordinary lantern has been designed and manufactured for exhibiting opaque objects, styled the "Aphengescope." These are made suitable for both single and double lanterns, the latter one giving the better results. It may be described as a box hexagonal in shape, two sides of which are provided with holes to receive the lights from the two lanterns, the objectives having been removed. On an intermediate side, between those in which the holes are made, is fixed an objective, and at the side opposite this objective the objects to be shown are placed; thus it will be noticed that the lanterns themselves are fixed with their backs opposite the screen, the light from both being united and concentrated to illuminate the object. On account of the great loss of light by reflection, large exhibitions with this adaptation should not be attempted.

STAND FOR THE LANTERN.

A USEFUL and convenient Stand for the Lantern is illustrated at Fig. 60. It consists of a tripod made of either ash or oak, upon which is fixed a board to which the lantern is attached. It possesses great steadiness, and is capable of adjustment to work at any height or angle, to suit the operator. In many instances it is desirable to have the lantern elevated to a considerable height from the floor, so as to bring the centre of the lantern in line with the centre of the screen. Thus, in showing a picture 12 feet in diameter, the bottom of which should not be less than 2 feet from the ground, the centres of the lantern would require to be 8 feet from the floor. This tripod is made when required with a ball-and-socket joint, placed between the flat table top and the top of tripod, also with other accessories

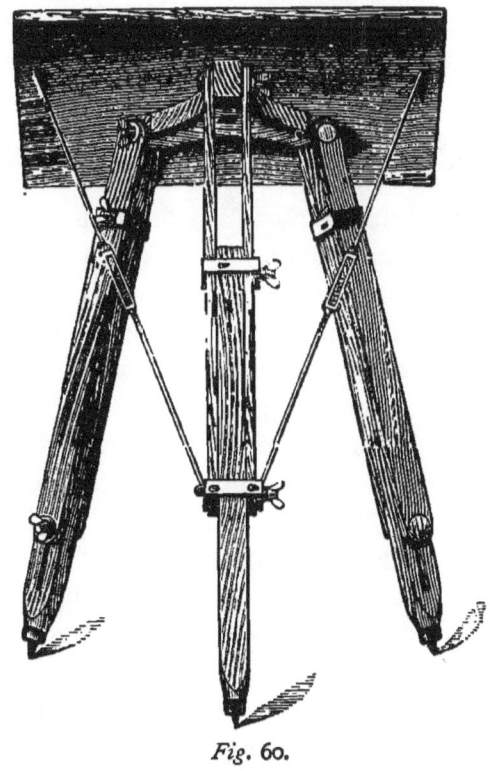

Fig. 60.

suitable for the photographer in supporting large cameras. It may also be adapted as a stand for supporting a telescope.

SCREENS.

IF a place can be assigned for a permanent Screen, nothing can surpass a whitened wall, which may be ornamented with drapery, or by a pair of Corinthian columns. These latter can be purchased at the decorator's or paper-hanger's, printed in colour ; and when varnished and fixed at each side of the screen, over the top of which a suitable inscription should be placed, forms an embellishment at a small outlay. By making a dead black border of some inches in width to the white screen, the pictures shown may overlap the border without being noticed, and thus every picture may be made to appear as registering absolutely.

In the case of Portable Screens, as the best results are to be derived from opaque ones, screens of this class may be obtained up to 10 feet square, made of cloth, faced with white paper having an ornamental border, the whole mounted upon a roller. This is a very convenient form, and is easy to erect ; but beyond the above dimensions they are altogether out of the range of portability. Those next in quality are of linen ; these also can be had up to 10 feet square, having no seams. As it is very objectionable to have a seam running down the centre of a screen, if a large one is required, it should be made by joining two pieces outside one wide width, so that the centre portion is free from piecings. A method adopted by the author for suspending linen screens of large dimensions in school-rooms, is to fix iron staples in the wall near to the ceiling, and also near to the floor. The screen being provided all round its edges with loops of tape, a sash-cord of suitable strength is threaded through the loops and also through the staples, whereby the whole is stretched perfectly tight and even. A length of fringe attached to the top, with a little drapery hanging down either side, gives a neat appearance without much trouble or cost.

A convenient form of portable frame for screens up to 12 feet is shown at Fig. 61. The frame is put together in the manner of a fishing-rod, and can be erected at private entertainments, without having to disturb furniture, etc., in an incredibly short time. It is, moreover, capable of being packed in a very small compass; another advantage being that it can be used as a Transparent Screen

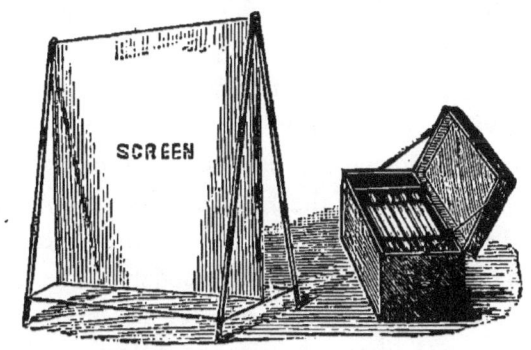

Fig. 61.

when occasion requires, the audience being placed on the opposite side to the lantern; but it should be remembered that by adopting this plan the result is never so good as with an opaque screen.

Transparent screens can be made of thin cotton sheeting, or, what is still better, of muslin. Before using they should be well wet with water; best applied after the screen is erected, by means of a garden syringe. This wetting makes the surface more homogeneous and transparent. A neat screen for exhibiting microscopic objects was constructed by the author, out of a child's wooden hoop about three feet in diameter, covered with tracing-paper, previously moistened, and then glued to its periphery. On becoming dry, it presented a beautifully even surface, and as tight as a drum.

By screwing a stick to the rim of the hoop it can be held in position, and regulated for height by tying to the back of a chair, or it may be fixed in the bottom portion of a photographer's head-rest stand.   Statuary exhibited upon this screen has a charming effect.

LANTERN SLIDES.

THE production of Photographic Magic Lantern Slides has been taken up, commercially, by some very enterprising firms in England, France, and America, the result being that complete series of views, at wonderfully low prices, are to be obtained, not only of our dear old country, but also of our much-prized India, the land of the Pharaohs, of the Holy Land, of the Alpine scenes of Switzerland, of the ruins of sunny Italy, of the bygone splendour and greatness of Spain, of the natural wonders of the Far West, of the Polar regions, of the Tropics ; and even the bowels of the earth have been photographed, as have also the fantastic and ever-changing forms of aërial grandeur ; whilst portraits of the sun, with the vast protuberance surrounding his edge, and the dark spots which travel across his face, together with eclipses, our satellite in all her phases, and the spectra of other heavenly bodies, though yet so far, are brought so near ; and the most minute details of insects and objects invisible to the unaided eye are produced in magnified dimensions with that correctness to which no living artist can aspire.   On looking at a photograph, we feel sure that we have a faithful representation of the subject, for the photographer has neither the power to add nor to detract from his subject.   He must, therefore, choose his point of sight with the skill which denotes the difference between a mere photographer and one who combines art with his profession.

The photographic transparencies in carbon, and known as the "Woodbury Lantern Slides," are among the finest ever produced. The process of their production admits of any colour, perhaps none more beautiful than the warm chocolate, for which these slides have obtained a world-wide reputation. They are printed from the choicest negatives of the most eminent photographic artists in the world : thus almost every slide in the long list published by the Sciopticon Company may be relied upon as a photographic gem. The shadows and darker portions are of a more transparent colour than in slides of which silver usually forms the deposit ; thus more light is allowed to pass through, and a more brilliant picture obtained on the screen. These slides are made 4¼ inches long by 3¼ deep, with a neat mount bearing the name of the subject, or, if desired, they are supplied 3¼ inches square (the English standard size).

The productions of Messrs. F. York and Son merit special praise. This firm devote themselves almost exclusively to lantern slides, and are, perhaps, the largest producers in the world. Their pictures of the animals in the collection of the Royal Zoological Society are really wonderful. The architectural views of London, and the more recent pictures of Paris and its Exhibition, are characteristic of the greatest ability. York's slides are produced by the wet collodion process, and toned with platinum, and therefore may be relied upon for permanency. They are of uniform size, 3¼ inches square, with circular mounts, having an aperture 2⅞ inches in diameter. Messrs. York print their slides up to the edges, thus giving the opportunity to those who would prefer to substitute any other shape of mount, square, cushion-shaped, or dome. On the edge of each slide is a printed label, bearing the title of the picture.

Messrs. Wilson, of Aberdeen, and Messrs. Valentine, of

Dundee, have always ranked amongst the highest class lantern slide producers; within the past few years, however, their business in this speciality has been so considerably augmented that special attention has been given to the subject, improvements have suggested themselves, and now there are very few slides, if any, that can excel those of Valentine's or Wilson's.

Mr. William England, whose fame is world wide known, has produced some of the finest lantern slides ever exhibited, and the perfection of his Statuary Slides is unsurpassed.

The French Slides of M. Levy (late Ferrier and Co.) and Messrs. Lachenell, of Paris, have long held a reputation for excellence; unlike most English Slides, these are produced on albumen dry plates, the exact formula of their production long being kept a secret.

It is supposed they were toned with sulphur, which, although it produces a most agreeable tone, is not always permanent. Photographs treated in this manner have been known to fade in a moderately short time, and leave behind but a shadow of their former beauty. The above firms have produced of late years many excellent lantern slides ; and as Stereoscopic Transparencies, it is much to be deplored, have not been so much in request as formerly, perhaps lantern slides may have occupied more of their attention.

A good stereoscopic slide does not always make a good lantern slide, as the latter usually requires less printing than is suitable for the stereoscope.

———

PRODUCTION OF PHOTOGRAPHIC SLIDES.

A LTHOUGH there are many lanternists who are also photographers, there are, perhaps, many who dread entering
into that art which brings up visions of soiled fingers, spoiled
clothes, dark rooms filled with a mass of apparatus and bottles
enough to fill a museum or chemist's shop, with unlimited expenditure. To such readers it may be well to give a few details on
the Production of Photographic Slides, so as to banish from their
minds all these ideas. Nowadays photography need not be made
the expensive, laborious, and tedious art of the past. Modern
improvements have placed it in the power of almost every tourist
to become a photographer, and for the production of lantern transparencies the whole apparatus, including pocket camera, chemicals,
dry plates, &c., may be kept in a box or cupboard, no dark room
being absolutely necessary, as all operations requiring the exclu-
sion of daylight can be performed in the evening. However, as
this treatise does not admit of a full description of photography,
we will suppose the reader to have acquired some knowledge of
the art from one of the many excellent modern works published
on the subject, and merely give an outline of a lengthened experience in the production of lantern transparencies. These may
be produced in several ways, by wet collodion, dry collodion,
albumen, or gelatine dry plates, and also by the carbon process.

To reply to the question, " Which is the best process for making
lantern transparencies ? " would be very difficult, as circumstances
and conditions, and the skill or experience of the operator, has
much to do with the matter. Perhaps the *simplest* plan for an

7

amateur is to print them upon gelatino-bromide plates, sold commercially by many firms who make a speciality of transparency plates, and supply the formula for developing same.

COLLODIO-BROMIDE EMULSION PROCESS,

as published by Mr. Wm. Brooks, is a favourite for amateurs who wish to produce the best results with little trouble.

` "*Cleaning the Plate.*—In my own practice for very many years I have never used anything for polishing the plate but methylated spirit. Before polishing, if the plates are dirty, I pass them through a hot bath of common washing soda, not allowing them to remain there longer than to soften and remove the dirt, old films, varnish, &c. A few minutes' immersion I find quite sufficient ; they are then taken out singly and washed rapidly under the tap, rubbing either with the fingers or a pad of rag, and freed from the soda solution as quickly as possible; for if any remains on the plate after drying, it is like so much grease, and rather difficult to get rid of. I never on any account use any of the mineral acids for cleaning plates, as I am sure they cause the film to slip, which is very troublesome. After the plates are dry, I rub over them methylated spirit, as before stated, and polish with a dry chamois leather kept expressly for the purpose. The plates, when polished, are taken singly on a pneumatic holder, and edged with indiarubber to the depth of about one-eighth of an inch all round; for this purpose I cut a camel-hair brush 'stumpy' with a pair of scissors, and tie a narrow slip of glass about an eighth of an inch wide on the side of it, allowing it to project a little below the hairs ; this acts as a guide. The indiarubber solution is made by dissolving the rubber in benzole.

"*Coating the Plate.*—The plate, when the edging is dry, is taken on a pneumatic holder, and the emulsion poured on from a bottle slowly and steadily, and the surplus poured off from one corner, and then set up to dry.*

"*Exposing the Plate.*—Undoubtedly the best results are obtained from small negatives exposed in contact; for lantern slides quarter-plate negatives are of very convenient size. The negative is placed in an ordinary printing frame, with rather weak springs, the emulsion plate ($3\frac{1}{4} \times 3\frac{1}{4}$) carefully laid on the negative, the back board placed in position under pressure of the springs. Great care must be taken that there is no grinding motion, or the film is at once spoiled; the pressure must be *direct*. In summer time, in diffused light, with an ordinary quality of printing negative, about one second exposure will be found sufficient; if the negative be dense, yellow, or green, the exposure has to be prolonged; a little practice is the best guide. If cold tones are required, short exposure must be given, and longer exposures if warm tones are desired.

"The exposure can be made in the camera by transmitting light in the ordinary way, when the image requires to be reduced from a large negative. To get the best result, the apparatus should be pointed to the sky; if the sun be shining, a piece of ground glass placed a few inches from the negative, to keep the texture of the glass out of focus, is all that is required. An exposure made in this way in a good average light may be from one minute upwards.

"*Development.*—After the plate has been exposed, methylated alcohol is poured over its surface and allowed to soak for one minute; care must be taken not to use the alcohol too strong, but it should be employed as strong as the film will allow, say, about 840.sg. The plate, after flooding with the alcohol, is placed in water. I generally use a basin—about half a gallon size—and drop the plate in face downwards; the con-

---

* The Washed Collodio-Bromide Emulsion may be made by many of the published formulas, or purchased from Mr. Brooks.

vexity of the basin does not allow the film to be injured in any way. While the alcohol is soaking out, the developer can be prepared, but before the latter is applied, the plate must be well washed, so that the water blends with the film, or the development will take place unevenly and in patches. There are many ways of accomplishing the development. I will first give the solutions :—

Solution P.

Pyrogallic acid	. 96 grains.
Absolute alcohol	. 1 ounce.

Five minims of the above will contain one grain of pyrogallic acid.

Solution A.

Carbonate of potassium . .	300 to 360 grains.
Bromide of potassium . . .	. 60 „
Acetate of soda . . . . ,	120 „
Water	. 12 ounces.

" Into a clean developing measure put—

Solution P.	. 10 to 20 minims.
Solution A. . . . . ˙ .	. 2 drachms.
Water	. 2 „

This is at once poured over the plate as soon as it is washed free from the alcohol.

"To obtain different ranges of tone I use, as will be seen, acetate of soda, but I do not always keep to that salt alone for the purpose, as various others can be used with advantage, namely, phosphate of soda, tungstate of soda, acetate of potash, citrate of soda and also of potash, and various others of a like nature. A few drops of a freshly-prepared saturated solution of borax added to the developer gives a very pretty tone. This solution appears to be a very powerful restrainer, so must be used with caution, but it loses its power if more than a day old.

"If the negative is weak the pyro requires to be increased; if dense and hard, it requires to be reduced.

"I always use cyanide of potassium as a fixing agent—about 20 grains to the ounce, or thereabouts—as it is more easily got rid of before toning; hpyo. gives no end of trouble. Should the image appear too dense and heavy after fixing, and before toning, I have ready about a 10-grain solution of cyanide, with about one drop of nitric acid added; this reduces the image very readily and evenly.

"After fixing allow to soak in a dish of clean water for about a quarter of an hour or more, and it is then ready for toning, which is readily accomplished with the following solution :—

Bichloride of platinum	1 grain.
Nitric acid	1 minim.
Water	3 ounces.

"A white porcelain dish is best for this purpose, if the plate has been properly exposed and developed. Almost any tone can be obtained as easily as in the case of the silver print.

"Should the image appear thin, it can easily be intensified before toning with—

Pyro	2 grains.
Citric acid	1 grain.
Water	1 ounce.

"With a drop or two of a 10-grain solution of nitrate of silver added, any amount of intensity can be obtained in this way, but care must be taken to avoid over-intensity. I have had all sorts of toning agents, but I find none of them to equal platinum."

TANNING PROCESS.

In this process a substratum is necessary to prevent the film from slipping off the plate during development. The following formula may be used without the necessity of polishing the plates; these after being well washed under a tap, should be slightly drained, and while still wet flowed over with

Albumen (white of egg) . . . . 1 ounce.

Water . . . . 1 pint.

Liquid ammonia . . . . . 15 drops.

This must be well shaken, either by means of an egg-beater, or in a bottle with some broken glass, and must be well filtered previous to using. After drying over a hot-water plate or before the fire, and allowed to cool, the plates are ready to receive the collodion, almost any good sample of which will do, preferably rather thick. Use an ordinary 45-grain silver bath, rather acid. After exciting the plate, wash well under a tap, and while wet apply the preservative solution, consisting of

Tannin . . . . . . 15 grains.

Water . . . , . . . 1 ounce.

Sugar. . . . . 5 grains.

This must be fresh mixed and well filtered.

The first application should be cast away, and a second applied. Now place in the drying-rack. The exposure is made by placing the plate *close* against a negative, the two film sides being in contact, any ordinary pressure printing-frame being used. The time of exposure varies according to the density of the negative, and the distance and nature of the light. However, with an ordinary negative, and placed some 6 inches away from the flame of an ordinary gas-burner, some 20 to 60 seconds will be required.

The development must be conducted in an equally non-actinic light to the preparation. First moisten the film by flowing over it a solution of alcohol and water in equal portions, now wash well, and the developing solution may be applied.

Pyrogallic acid . . . . 3 grains ⎱ mixed fresh.
Water . . . . . 1 ounce ⎰

This will soon cause the image to appear if the exposure has been properly timed; and when sufficient detail is manifest re-develop with same solution, with the addition of a few drops.

Citric acid	30 grains.
Nitrate of silver	20 grains.
Water, ...	ounces.

This will soon bring the picture to the necessary depth. It should now be washed and fixed in

Hyposulphite of soda . .	1 ounce,
Water	6 ounces,

when, after further washing, the picture is finished, and should be of a good warm tone. If necessary, it may be toned with a weak solution of chloride of gold.

MODIFIED ALBUMEN PROCESS.

By this process the best possible results can be obtained. Take a good bromo-iodized collodion, which must be old and ripe, and in such condition that as soon as it is set it may be written upon with a pen without tearing the film. After coating the plate, when set it must be immersed in water for a few minutes, and then well washed under a gentle stream from the tap. Now coat with albu-men as follows :—

Albumen (from fresh eggs)	10 ounces.
Acetic acid	1½ drams.

Previous to mixing, the albumen should be beaten into a froth. Stir well with a glass rod, and allow to stand for twelve hours, then strain through muslin or sponge, and add 40 drops of strong liquid ammonia. In 6 drams of water dissolve 60 grains of iodide of ammonium and 10 grains of bromide of ammonium. Now add this solution to the filtered albumen, allow this to soak into the film for a minute or two, then set it to drain, and dry in a warm place. To excite, the plate must be allowed to remain forty seconds or not more than a minute in a bath made as follows:—

Nitrate of silver	1 ounce.
Distilled water	8 ounces.
Acetic acid	2 ounces.

Now rinse the plate well under a tap for one or two minutes, and set aside to dry. When dry, the back of the plate must be coated with burnt sienna finely ground, with a little gum-water added.

Exposure.—From five seconds to five minutes, depending upon the intensity of the negative and the quality of the light.

Development.—After removing from the printing-frame, rinse the plate under the tap and clear away the backing, best done with a piece of spongy india-rubber. The development is best conducted in a flat dish, which may be made of a piece of ribbed glass and a well-varnished wooden frame, and need not be much larger than the plate itself.

P	Pyrogallic acid	60 grains.
	Glacial acetic acid	2 ounces.
	Water	20 ounces.
	Citric acid	10 grains.
S	Nitrate of silver	20 grains.
	Water	1 ounce.

Take of solution P sufficient to cover the plate, and warm it in a beaker to about 140 degrees Fahrenheit; pour this over the plate, keeping it in motion for about a minute, then add three drops of solution S, still keeping the plate in motion. In a short time the shadows will begin to appear. As soon as they are visible by transmitted light, wash well, and gently rub and polish well the film with a tuft of cotton wool. Now proceed with P moderately hot, and add a few drops of S. So soon as the required density is attained, wash well and again polish with cotton wool.   Fix in

Hyposulphite of soda , .	6 ounces.
Water . . . , .	1 pint.

to which must be added

Chloride of gold	4 grains.
Water . . . . , . .	2 ounces.

The plate must remain in the fixing solution fifteen to twenty minutes, being rocked occasionally, and when removed, well washed.

The most important condition to the success of this process is to have the collodion right, and although the iodides and bromides are washed out, it must not be supposed that plain uniodized collodion will answer the purpose.   The plate after being excited should present an uniform slight blue tinge : if of a patchy or mottled appearance, the collodion is too horny.   No varnishing will be required.

CARBON TRANSPARENCIES.

Perhaps no process suits the requirements of the amateur better than the Carbon Process for the production of Lantern Transparencies.   A special tissue for this purpose is prepared by the Autotype Company, of a dense warm black.   It may be had either sensitized or unsensitized, and in the latter state will keep for an almost indefinite period.   The method of sensitizing is as follows:—

A solution of bichromate of potash is made by dissolving one part of this salt in twenty to thirty parts of water.   This is poured into a tin dish, and the tissue *immersed*, face downwards, until it becomes perfectly pliable (care being taken to exclude any air-bubbles), which will generally take thirty or forty seconds, but in winter as much as two minutes may be requisite.   In summer it is sometimes requisite to keep a piece of ice in one corner of the tin dish. The tissue on being removed is placed face downwards on a sheet of glass, which may be previously wetted with sensitizer. A squeegee is now passed over the back to remove all excess of solution taken up by the paper. On removing from the glass plate, the tissue will be found to present an uniformly clear surface. It must now be hung up to dry. As much depends upon the drying, amateurs whose requirements are small would do well to purchase the tissue ready sensitized.

The glass plates on which the transparency is to rest should be prepared by coating with

Gelatine .   .   .   .   .   1 ounce.
Water   .   .   .   . 10 ounces.
Chrome alum .   .   .   .   . 10 grains.

This must be caused to flow over like collodion, and, if necessary, be guided to the edges of the plate by a glass rod. The plates may now be reared up, and when dry are ready for use.

These will keep any length of time, so they may be prepared beforehand.

To Print.—A thin black paper mask must be placed upon the negative, the aperture in which being a little less than the glass plate, and to include as much of the picture as wished. The object of this mask is to procure what is termed a "safe-edge." The sensitized tissue, already cut to the size, is now laid upon the masked negative and printed in a pressure-frame. A little longer exposure will be usually required than would be necessary with sensitized albumenized paper. The exposed tissue is now removed, and immersed face down in a dish of cold water. It will immediately curl up, but will in a few seconds lie perfectly flat in the water. At this stage slip one of the prepared glasses into the dish, and bring its gelatinized surface directly under the tissue; draw the two out of the water together, and apply the squeegee to the back. As many as are printed may be treated in a similar manner, and placed one on the top of the other to keep them flat. The underneath one may now be developed by placing it in water of the temperature of 80 to 90 degrees Fahrenheit, and shortly the paper forming the backing to the tissue will curl away. A dark slimy mass will now be perceived on the glass plate, and by gently moving the plate in the warm water the soluble portions will clear away, leaving the insoluble portions attached to the glass plate.

Should the transparency appear too light, deficient in half-tone, and without depth in the shadows, it is a sign of under-exposure ; should it be over-exposed, it will be dark and indistinct, and the gelatine, of which the tissue is formed, difficult to dissolve away, in which case increase the temperature of the water. The remedy for under or over-exposure is decrease or increase in temperature of the water, warmer water being necessary for over-exposure, and colder for under-exposure. So soon as sufficiently developed, immerse for five minutes in a bath of

| Alum | . | . | . | . | . | . | 1 part. |
| Water | . | . | . | . | . | . | 40 parts. |

Wash well, and after drying, mount in the usual way. Ordinary printing negatives are more suitable for carbon printing than the thin ones often used in transparency printing.

Should the prints not be sufficiently dark or vigorous, they may be intensified like an ordinary wet collodion negative, or immersed in a bath of protosulphate of iron and gallic acid.

Although a fair outline of the process is here given, for further particulars the reader is referred to the "Autotype Company's Manual," popular edition, or to the excellent publication, "A Manual of the Carbon Process," by Dr. Paul Liesegang, translated from the German by Mr. R. B. Marston.

WET COLLODION PROCESS.

Up to now the making of photographic transparencies for the lantern has been treated upon dry plates, or such as can be exposed in contact with the negative, and, with the exception of the carbon process, all the operations of preparation, exposing, and developing can be performed in the evening, therefore no dark room or day-light being absolutely necessary. But in the wet collodion process a camera and lens are indispensable, and a dark room for developing, and daylight for exposing, essential. There are many modifications of the wet collodion process, but the one to be described has been worked out specially for lantern slides by Mr. John S. Pollitt, of Manchester, who has succeeded by it in producing some of the most charming results ever seen on the screen, and at a recent exhibition of slides, made by more than a dozen different processes, by as many or more exhibitors, the wet collodion (by this process) bore the palm. The negative to be copied should be soft and full of detail; it may be of any size, those of large size, say 12 by 10 inches, being as convenient as stereoscopic size. A camera and lens of ordinary construction will answer the requirements. The negative may be fixed in a window, with a sheet of white paper placed on a board, adjustable to the proper angle so as to reflect a uniform light on to the negative, and, unless the negative be very intense, all diffused light should be excluded from the front. A good bromo-iodized collodion should be used, which is better for being old and ripe and not too heavily iodized; if thick, it should be diluted with ether s.p. 7·25. An ordinary silver bath should be employed, made decidedly acid with a drop or two of glacial acetic acid. Great care must be exercised in focussing, and a small stop should be inserted in the lens.

To develope the plate, the following solutions are necessary, and as the superiority of the process depends almost entirely upon the development, care must be exercised and exact adherence of the formula observed :—

A {
In a large earthenware jar, add one ounce of sulphuric acid to three ounces of water (heat will be generated.) When cold, add one ounce of the best gelatine (Nelson's.) Allow this to swell for some time, after which place the jar and its contents in a warm place for twenty-four hours, say, at a temperature not exceeding 100 degrees Fahrenheit, when the gelatine will be found dissolved. Next add clean iron filings in excess, avoiding any application of heat. At this stage allow the whole to stand for several days, then add fifteen ounces of a two-grain (to the ounce) solution of acetate of soda. The whole may now be filtered and bottled for future use, and in this condition will keep good indefinitely.

B* {
To thirty ounces of water, add one ounce of proto-sulphate of iron and four drachms of glacial acetic acid.

To develope the transparency take sufficient (to cover the plate) of B solution in a glass developing cup, and add a few drops of A solution (the quantity of A may be regulated by the amount of vigour it is desired to produce in the resulting image), flow it over the plate in the usual way, and if the image appears quickly, indicating full exposure, the developer should be poured off, and the plate exposed for a little time to the action of the atmosphere in the dark room, which if the exposure has not been overdone, brings out the picture with great brilliancy. When the image is well out, wash thoroughly, and fix with cyanide of potassium.

The above developer acts somewhat slowly compared with other

---

* This solution will keep good for four or six months, but not longer.

iron developers, but, when a suitable *ripe* collodion be used, gives an exceedingly fine deposit of reduced silver in the film, and thus the picture is admirably suited for enlargement or projection.

It is better with a view to clearness and brilliancy to expose fully, and so cause the developer to act as quickly as possible. If, however, after fixing, the image is found to lack density, the plate must be washed well and intensified with a three-grain solution of pyrogallic acid, acidulated with one drachm of glacial acetic acid, and a few drops of a thirty-grain solution of silver nitrate.

This application usually produces a beautiful warm tone, well suited to lantern transparencies.

If it be desired to tone the transparency, so as to darken the colour by reflected light, a very weak solution of a mixture of gold chloride and potassium chloride applied to the film, will produce the desired effect; when dry, the transparency may be mounted without varnishing, but if a good clear coat of transparent varnish can be applied, without streaks, the brilliancy will be improved: however, as this is a part where many amateurs fail, a thin coating of albumen may be substituted.

MOUNTING OF LANTERN SLIDES.

LANTERN SLIDES should always be protected by a plain glass in front, with a paper mount between the glass and the picture of a suitable shape,—either round, cushion-shaped, or dome. A good plan is to have these mounts black on one side and white on the other, the white side being convenient for writing the name of the picture, and should be next the plain glass, so that when exhibiting it may be easily seen; thus by adopting one regular system of placing the white side next the condenser the pictures will always appear the natural way on the screen. This latter is important, more especially in the case of a slide which exhibits a clock or a printed sign. The mounts for the purpose are most easily cut by using the "Photographic Trimmer" (Fig. 62), and the shapes for same (Figs. 63, 64, 65, and 66), which latter may be procured in a variety of forms and sizes. With this little instrument the smallest curves and circles may

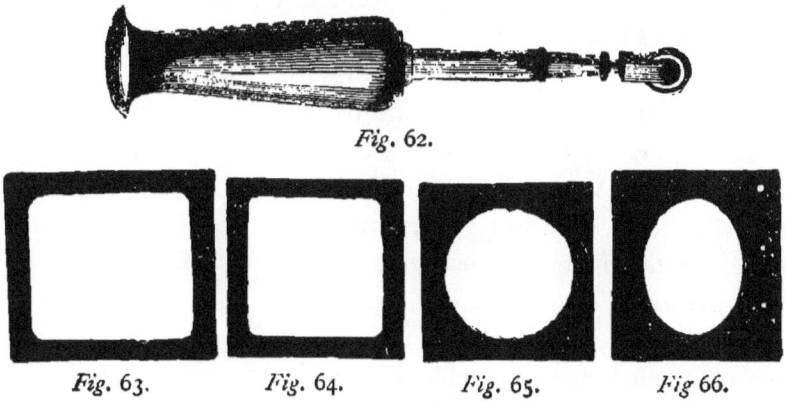

Fig. 62.

Fig. 63.   *Fig.* 64.   *Fig.* 65.   *Fig* 66.

be cut as clean and sharp as possible to imagine, the only instructions necessary being to keep the cutter pressed well up to the inside edge of the mount, and with one sweep to go round the whole. A sheet of zinc forms an excellent medium for cutting upon. The edges of the slide should be bound with paper, the best for the purpose being the sort in which needles are wrapped, and known commercially as "needle" paper. Gelatine or gum tragacanth are good adhesive mediums.

The old-fashioned method of mounting slides in wood frames should be abolished, as not only is the expense greater, but they take up much more room for storage, and are less portable; moreover, unless stopping-pieces are attached, arranged to the width of the slide stage of lanterns (which unfortunately are not always alike), the pictures will be far from registering on the screen; whereas, by dispensing with the wood frames, no greater liability to breakage is incurred, and they may be used by means of a suitable carrier in any lantern, by this means giving absolute registration. As some of our readers may not understand the benefit of correct registration, a few words on the subject may not be out of place. What is meant by correct registration is that when dissolving one picture away, the following one should take its place identically, and without any alteration in the margin of the picture being observed. Let us take the picture of a landscape in summer, in which a cottage, trees, etc., may be present, dissolving into one of the same subject identically, but in winter-time. The two should be so dissolved that one takes up the place of the other exactly, the transformation being effected without the observers becoming aware of the change taking place until the effect is actually attained. Should the registration be neglected, the second picture most probably will make its appearance out of place, and there will be seen a double picture, until such time as the operator has moved the slide into its proper place. This shifting of slides when once on the screen mars the whole effect, and in many instances has the writer known this want of registration to spoil what would have been an enjoyable entertainment.

CARRIERS.

IT is a pity that all lantern slide producers could not have agreed upon one definite size as a standard. As it is, some make them $3\frac{1}{4}$ square, others $4\frac{1}{4} \times 3\frac{1}{4}$, and the French size being $3\frac{7}{8} \times 3\frac{1}{4}$, while many amateurs make the slides out of stereoscopic plates cut in halves, namely, $3\frac{3}{8} \times 3\frac{1}{4}$. All seem to have adopted the $3\frac{1}{4}$ in depth, therefore the most practical form of Carriers are those in which the pictures are slided through. Thus, one having been placed in the carrier, a second one is introduced, which pushes the previous one into its place; a third one now pushes the second into position, and simultaneously projects the first one to the outer end of the carrier, so that it may be removed. The slideholder shown at Fig. 67 is intended for pictures to be passed through it in a panoramic fashion, but as the slides are carried on a piece of tape placed round two small pulleys, the movement is apt to be very unsteady; moreover, the mounts forming

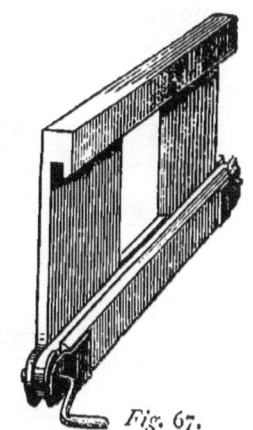

Fig. 67.

the margins of the pictures in passing through present to the eye an unseemly black patch, increased the more by the ends of two pictures being together.

REGISTERING CARRIER.

A Registering Carrier was some time ago introduced by the author, in which slides of all the usual sizes could be used indiscriminately with perfect registration. A description of the same was published in the *British Journal Photographic Almanac*, and is here reproduced (Fig. 68).

"Some time ago I went to an exhibition of dissolving views given by a friend. He had a most elaborate apparatus and some good views, but they were badly exhibited. The first picture shown, after being set in position, looked very well; the second made its appearance some two or three feet out of its intended position, and had to be moved during the dissolving; the third came on similar to the second, considerably out of place; and during the whole of the exhibition the pictures had to be adjusted during dissolving. Sometimes there would be a round picture, then a cushion-shaped, and afterwards a dome, causing an everlasting shifting about, which, added to the noise of the carriers being re-

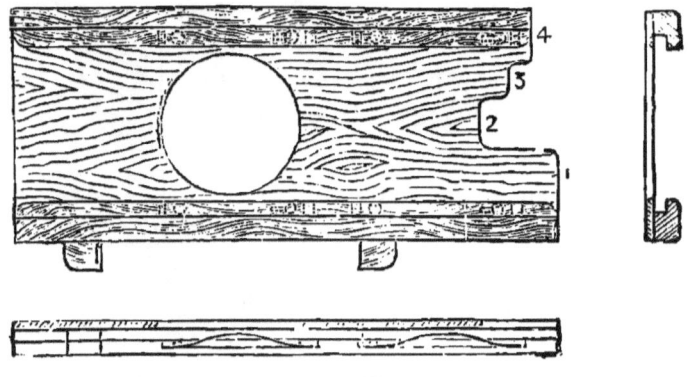

Fig. 68.

moved and replaced in the lanterns, very much detracted from the enjoyment of the evening. I was quite disappointed at the management of my lantern friend. At the close of the exhibition I remarked, 'You ought to register your pictures better on the screen.' He seemed to make light of the matter, therefore I invited him to spend an evening with me, and I would show him how I obtained a far better result with much less noise and trouble. On the appointed evening my friend arrived, and after a little refreshment we retired to the room where I usually exhibit my lanterns. In a few minutes I had my Sciopticons at work, using oil.

"'What a splendid light you get!' said my friend. 'I have

never seen so good a light before with the same apparatus. How do you produce it?'

"'Simply by good oil, wicks properly cut and trimmed, lenses clean, and an opaque screen faced with white paper.'

"'And what a beautiful picture that is!' said he: 'America, isn't it?'

"'Yes.'

"'Whose slide is it?'

"'Woodbury's.'

"'It's very nice, but I don't like the size' ($3\frac{1}{4} \times 4\frac{1}{4}$). 'I have bother enough with slides of different sizes already, and I don't care to introduce another.'

"'Well,' I replied, 'I think the Woodbury slide the best size, and can give you many reasons for it. One is that you have only one chance of getting the picture the wrong way, whereas in the square slide the chances are three to one. However, let us go on.'

"My second picture came on very nicely.

"'That's good, too,' said my friend. 'Is that a Woodbury slide?'

"'No, it's York's' ($3\frac{1}{4} \times 3\frac{1}{4}$). So I varied by putting in a square slide, then a Woodbury, changing them about indiscriminately for some eight or nine pictures, when my friend turned round, remarking,

"'How beautifully they dissolve, and how accurately they register! There is not the slightest alteration in the margin, notwithstanding you use slides of different sizes every time' (which I did purposely). 'How do you manage it?'

"'By means of my carriers, which are fixtures in the lanterns, the aperture in them forming the margin of the picture, being slightly less than the paper mount inside the slide; and both carriers being exactly alike, the pictures are simply passed through.

Also on the carriers I have different lengths, or stopping-edges, suitable for the different sizes of slides.' (This the accompanying drawing will show).

"My friend was so highly pleased with the carriers that he ordered a pair the next day. I have shown them to many lantern friends, who all acknowledge their simplicity and efficiency. I shall be glad to see any improvements that your readers may suggest. It will be seen from the drawing how the carrier is applied. In placing a picture into the carrier to start with, it needs no fixed stop; the second picture, according to its size and that of the first one, must be pushed to one or other of the stopping-edges, by which means the first picture will be pushed into its right position in the centre of the disc. Thus, suppose the first picture to be $3\frac{1}{4} \times 3\frac{1}{4}$, and the second to be $3\frac{1}{4} \times 3\frac{1}{4}$, use Stop No. 2. Now, suppose the first picture to be $3\frac{1}{4} \times 4\frac{1}{4}$ (Woodbury size), and the second picture the same size, use No. 1, or, as I always remember it, the longest slide and the longest stop, also the shortest slide and the shortest stop; and suppose you use a Ferrier size, stop No. 4; in case you have $3\frac{1}{4} \times 3\frac{1}{4}$ in the carrier, and the next picture is $3\frac{1}{4} \times 4\frac{1}{4}$, use also Stop No. 4; in case you have a Woodbury slide in the carrier, and have $3\frac{1}{4} \times 3\frac{1}{4}$ following, use Stop No. 3. Although this may seem a little complicated at first to some as I have explained it, I can assure you in practice it is very simple. It will be seen from the diagram that the grooves are very wide, suitable for the thickest slide, and by having two little springs arranged in the grooves at the top and bottom, the pictures are always kept in one definite position, preventing the passage of one slide over the other, or the possibility of two slides getting locked, as is often the case with thin French slides. Another advantage is that after once focussing, readjustment is seldom, if ever, required."

Although this is the best form of "push through" Carrier, and

most suitable for a single lantern, or for even a small Biunial
Lantern, it has a great disadvantage, when using it with a large

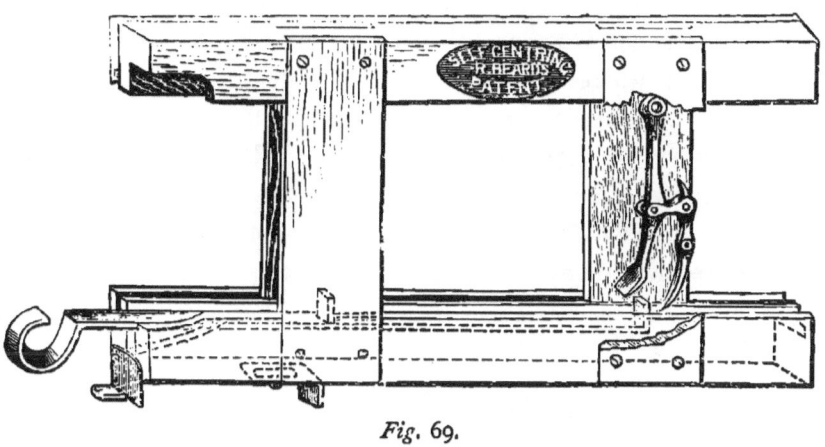

Fig. 69.

lantern, by requiring both hands when changing slides—one to
push in the new slide and the other to take out the exhibited

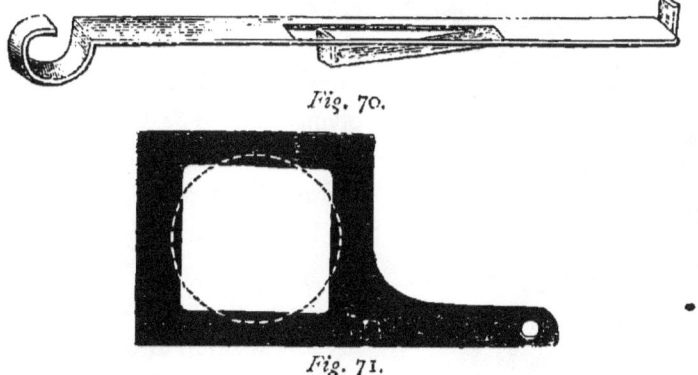

Fig. 70.

Fig. 71.

slide at the opposite side of the lantern.   This drawback is overcome by the ingenious Self-registering Carrier of Mr. Beard shown
at Fig. 69.

The writer has had a set of three of these carriers in use with his Triple Lantern for some time, and no hesitation in saying that, when well made, they are the best carriers for automatically registering slides of various sizes ever used with the lantern. It matters not, whatever be the length of slide, from 3 inches to $4\frac{1}{4}$ inches, it becomes automatically centred on being placed on the brass runner, Fig. 70, and pushed home. Each carrier is provided with two metal masks, Fig. 71, which are made to slide in grooves immediately behind the photograph, and thus ensures perfect registration at the margin of the disc.

STATUARY.

SCARCELY any subject of photography can be shown on the screen to excel that of Statuary. In many cases these are stopped out with Indian-ink, and nothing is seen but the simple

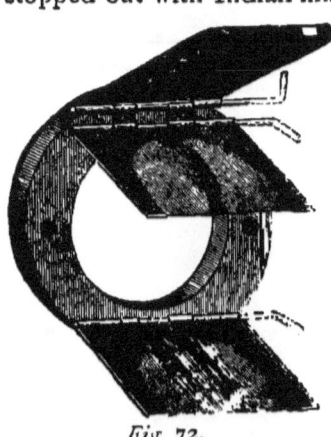

Fig. 72.

statue upon a black ground in bold relief. One very effective way to exhibit this class of slide by a dissolving lantern is to dissolve them into blue glass. This is done as follows : First place a blue glass in one lantern (sheets of coloured gelatine will answer the same purpose, and may be made to any required depth of shade), and through it project a disc on to the screen. A statuary slide is now placed in the other lantern, and the dissolving conducted very slowly until the statue appears in full, with the shadow portions a deep blue in comparison with the lighter parts; now gently dissolve back again, leaving the blue disc; change the picture, and proceed as before.

Another way of exhibiting statuary slides is by means of two slide tinters (shown at Fig. 72). These consist of flanges fitted to the front parts of the objectives, on which are fixed metallic frames, each holding a sheet of thin coloured gelatine; an opaque shutter is also attached to each, for application when it is necessary for the lanterns to remain in darkness. The method of procedure is this : Project a picture on the screen through the gelatine; now gently raise the frame holding the gelatine until the picture has increased much in brightness; then gradually lower the frame. With the second lantern a similar operation will be performed; so that, while dissolving one picture into the other, both frames will be down.

The slide tinter is very useful for a variety of effects, such as sunsets, moonlights, etc.; also for giving to ordinary photographs, in many cases, the effect of a coloured slide, by the judicious application of different coloured sheets of gelatine for sky and foreground. These different sheets may be introduced into the frame at will.

Superior to the slide tinters fixed upon the nozzles of the objectives are sheets of coloured glass inserted between the light and the condenser, by means of apertures cut in the body of the lantern, and closed when not in use by polished brass doors.

Another novel effect when exhibiting statuary, is by means of the roller curtain shutter, described at page 121.

COLOURING OF SLIDES.

IN the Colouring of Slides for Magic Lantern purposes the greatest care is necessary, and considerable practice is required ere anything like a favourable result can be achieved. The best light by which to operate is lamp or gaslight. This is a benefit to the amateur, whose time during the day is perhaps fully occupied with matters pertaining to £ s. d., and therefore could not devote so much daytime to the subject as would insure success.

Colours in both oil and water are used to obtain the best results, where richness, depth, brilliancy, and force of effect are desired.

Fig. 73.

It should be remembered that none but transparent colours must be used. These can be purchased from most artists' colourmen, ready arranged in boxes with all the requisite materials for painting on glass, such as "fixings," palette, palette-knife, leather dabbers, turpentine, mastic-varnish, pale drying-oil, and gold size, etc. A large number of brushes are necessary—one for each kind of colour used in oil or water of the different tints. The next thing required is a suitable desk or easel, with a glass back, as shown in Fig. 73. The slide to be coloured should be perfectly clear in the transparent parts, and not too cold in tone. It should not be over printed, as in that case there would be a want of vigour and contrast; and as the colourist can strengthen foregrounds and other objects of detail, or throw back those wanting in relief or gradation, a slightly under-exposed print is to be preferred. Still, much will depend upon the nature of the subject, as, for instance, where a wide' gloomy, and desolate effect is sought, a slightly over printed slide will be better; and where a wide expanse of country, with distant mountains, is desired, a soft, delicate print will aid the artistic colourist in securing air and light. If buildings and figures are to be the principle objects, the print should be correctly exposed, as if to be shown without any colour.

We commence first with the water-colour, by mixing on the palette such colours as Prussian blue, burnt sienna, crimson lake, and yellow to some of the numerous compounds, ranging through browns, purples, greens, and neutral tints to a very powerful transparent black, to each of which a little ox-gall should be added.

Proceed by strengthening the masses of the deeper shadows, the markings and cast shadows of the foreground, etc. A full brush should be used, and the colour applied in an even wash. The colour should not be too strong, or the edges of the wash will be disagreeably visible. If, however, the wash is too strong, apply the action of the breath, and whilst still moist, go over it with a flat camel's-hair brush. No attempt must be made to apply a second colour until the first is quite dry. Should the part require strengthening, another light wash may be applied, and thus any depth of colour may be obtained. Foreground objects should be made to stand forward more prominently, and the masses of foliage made distinctly visible.

Before applying what are called *local* colours, it is well to apply a very thin coat of transparent enamel varnish over those already applied. When this is dry the local colouring can be proceeded with, and may be carried over all the parts except the high lights and sky, which are reserved for oil or varnish colours specially prepared for the purpose, as previously stated. These (to be effective) require more skill in using than water-colours. The brushes are similar to those used with the water-colours, with the addition of a few hog's-hair tools and a dabber, made from an old white kid glove, by stuffing a piece of the kid with cotton-wool. In proceeding with the sky the hog's-hair brush is used, held perpendicular, and the colour dabbed or stippled on, after which a broad camel's-hair brush is swept over the surface to make the colours smooth. The dabber is next used to make it still more even. For the smaller surfaces, such as the high lights in distant mountains, &c., a sable brush may be used with advantage. These colours may be thinned with a little turpentine and a small portion of dryers and gold size added.

To facilitate the drying, heat may be applied, which is best done upon a small iron plate under which a gaslight or small Brunsen's burner is fixed. The greatest care must be taken to avoid dust, and no brush used for two colours without previously cleansing.

The principles of art, which guide the painter on canvas or paper, apply equally to transparency colouring. The *highest* light, deepest shadow, and brightest colours occur in the foreground; in the middle distance the colours lose their force, and in the extreme distance the colours should be used still less forcibly or in lighter tints, remembering that blue is the coldest colour and the most retiring, and therefore should predominate in the distant parts of the landscape. Red is warmer in colour, and is more used in combination for the nearer compositions, and adds considerable force in foregrounds, buildings, figures, &c. Orange and yellows may be used with discretion in nearer objects and foregrounds. Yellow, being the lightest of colours, should occur in the brightest parts of the picture.

Daylight effects should be kept warm in tone; moonlights, cold.

Fig. 74.

Before attempting to colour photograph transparencies, the amateur should practice upon a few of the outlines printed upon glass, as at Fig. 74. These are sold by many of the artists' colourmen and lantern slide dealers.

EFFECT SLIDES.

IN using Effect Slides, two or more lanterns are necessary, These slides are usually hand painted, although, of late, photography has been turned to good account in this direction, and, notwithstanding the extra care and trouble in their prepara tion, they amply repay for this expenditure.

 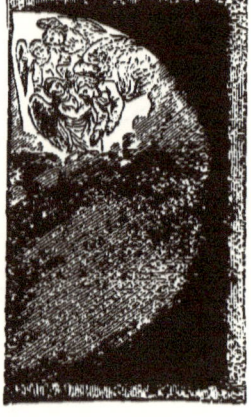

Fig. 75.   Fig. 76.

Some very wonderful effects can be produced : among these are the change from day to night, summer to winter, the formation of rainbows, tempests at sea, with shipwrecks and lightning, the storming of forts, etc.

To more clearly illustrate the object of effect slides, let us de scribe an exhibition of a set of slides called the "Orphan's Dream." This set consists of two slides (Figs. 75 and 76). In one lantern is placed the foundation slide (Fig. 75), representing a child asleep upon a couch, and in the other lantern is placed the *effect* slide

(Fig. 76). First the foundation slide is displayed; and then, on commencing the dissolving, the effect will be made to appear gradually and then disappear.

Messrs. F. York and Son have produced many beautifully-arranged effect slides, illustrating some of the works of the late Charles Dickens—"Gabriel Grub," "The Christmas Carol," also "The Pilgrim's Progress," "How Jane Conquest Rang the Bell," and many others—all from life models.

In cases where several effects follow alternately, two lanterns may be used, by placing the foundation picture in one, and dissolving the *effects* alternately in the other lantern; but by far the best plan is to use three lanterns, and by this means the dissolving is made perfect. Thus, in the slides of the "Soldier's Dream," the principal or foundation slide represents a soldier fallen asleep on the battle-field, beside the camp fire. He is supposed to be dreaming, and the vision of a happy home is caused to appear in the smoke of the camp fire by means of a second lantern; now this vision is changed to one of departure for war, and followed by engagements on the battle-field, and victory in the end. It will be seen that the foundation slide must remain on the screen the whole time, and will therefore occupy one lantern. The first effect slide must be placed in the second lantern, and made to appear; the second effect slide must be placed in the third lantern, and by these two latter lanterns the effects may be dissolved without interfering with the foundation slide.

In some effects even more than three lanterns are required, and at the Royal Polytechnic Institution as many as six lanterns have been in use at one time for the production of effects, such as the Siege of Delhi, in which the fire of artillery, the bursting of shells, etc., are portrayed. Four lanterns were most frequently used at the above institution. An illustration (Fig. 77) shows before and

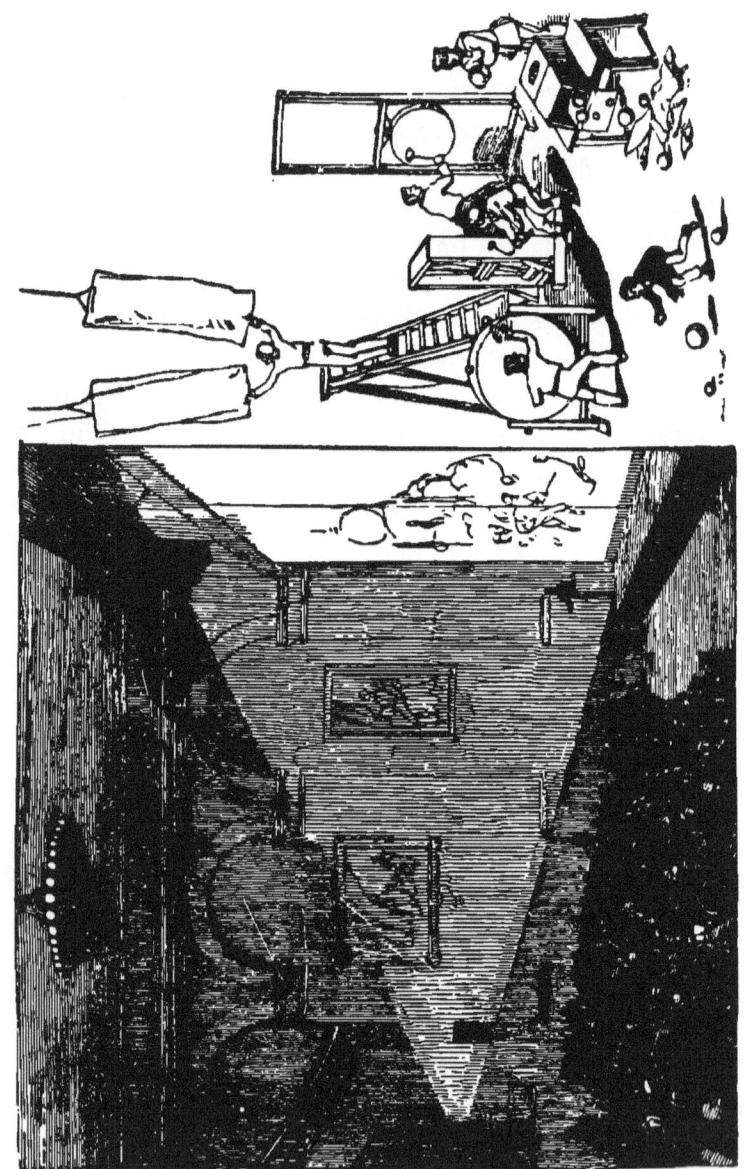

Fig. 77.

behind the scenes at the same institution during a lantern exhibition of the above description, and is taken from Professor Pepper's "Play-book of Science," by permission of the publishers.*

"The optical effects were assisted by various sounds in imitation of war's alarms, for the production of which more *volunteers* than were absolutely required would occasionally trespass behind the scenes, and produce those terrific sounds that some persons of a nervous temperament said were really *stunning.*"

MECHANICAL SLIDES.

THE above embrace a variety of scientific as well as comic slides, and no class of picture can be made more entertaining or instructive than a really good set of Astronomical Slides. Among this class comes the *Roller Curtain Slide and Shutter.* This is one of the most novel additions to modern lanterns, and no first-class instrument is made without it. The effect is generally produced at the opening of an exhibition, when the first slide, *a curtain* (either hand painted or photographic), arranged to imitate a theatrical drop scene, with all the necessary tassels, cords, valences, etc., occasionally an appropriate inscription or a device, forming a centrepiece.

This curtain is to be rolled up, displaying the view as if it were under the curtain, and by its use statuary slides are shown in a very pleasing manner. The shutter used in connection with the curtain slide consists of a stout sheet of brass, exactly the length from centre to centre of the optical systems, placed between the condensers and the slide when in position, and so arranged that

---

* See also Professor Pepper's more advanced work, "Cyclopædic Science Simplified."

by side pieces sliding in grooves it may be drawn up from the top, as shown in position in Fig. 55. To use it in a Biunial Lantern the curtain slide must be placed in the bottom lantern, and as the shutter is raised the uncovering of the slide has the appearance of rolling the curtain down on the sheet. The view to be shown, or the statuary, is introduced in the top lantern, and the light turned on to both. The shutter covering the top slide, no light is allowed to pass until the shutter is pushed down, which, if of the correct length, will cover the lower portion of the curtain, and uncover the lower part of the view at the same time. If statuary be shown this way, the curtain should be lowered again, another slide substituted, and proceeded with as before.

With a triple lantern a pair of side curtains, thrown on with the bottom lantern, and kept there all the time statuary is being exhibited, still further increases the effect, and is very beautiful. In this case the centre curtain is masked to fit inside the side curtains.

The same apparatus may be used occasionally to advantage, instead of dissolving ; and if, in course of a lecture, a map is to be shown, it should be rolled down and up again, as the curtain was.

A beautiful mechanical effect is produced by the rackwork slide, the CHROMATROPE (Fig. 79). This was invented by Mr. Childe, the inventor of dissolving views. It consists of two discs of glass painted in brilliant transparent colours, generally radiating from the centre to the outside, and forming, when placed face to face, the reverse of each other. The handle on being turned gives a rotary motion to the glass discs in opposite directions. The result is an ever-varied change of design and colour.

A great variety of designs can be adapted to the same mechanical arrangement for displaying geometrical and chromatic effects. Two pieces of perforated zinc introduced give some very extraordinary

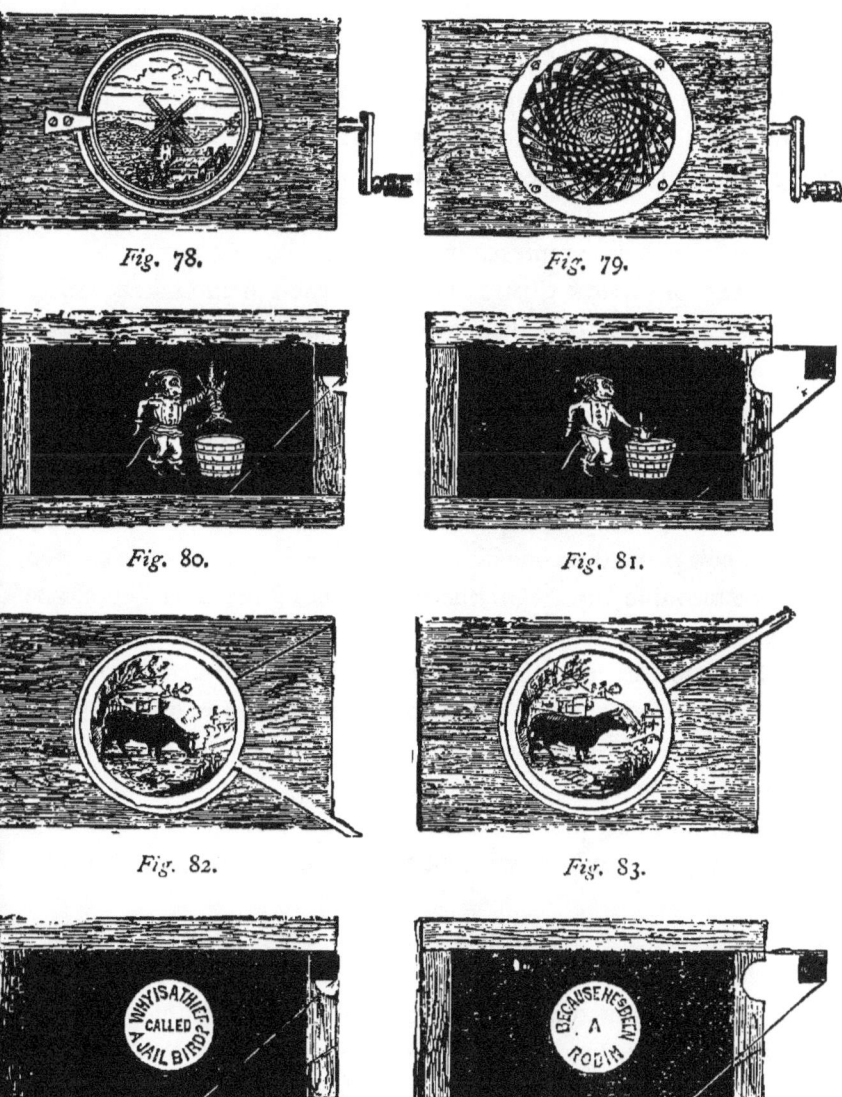

Fig. 78.

Fig. 79.

Fig. 80.

Fig. 81.

Fig. 82.

Fig. 83.

Fig. 84.

Fig. 85.

geometrical effects, also two pieces of wire gauze give a variety of designs of the watered silk type. .

The Windmill (Fig. 78) is another rackwork slide. In this case only one disc is caused to revolve, that one on which the sails of the mill only are painted, the landscape being painted on a fixed disc. Similar to this is a slide of a mill with the water-wheel in motion, also a slide representing a man swallowing rats.

TRANSFORMATION COMIC SLIDES are made in an endless variety of subjects. The one illustrated at Figs. 80 and 81 represents a wicked monkey, who, having caught a cat, persists in dipping pussy over head in the water-tub.

LEVER SLIDES (Figs. 82 and 83) are made of two discs, one of which only is made movable. Thus, for instance, one representing a cow having come down to the water to drink, has the body only of the cow painted on one disc, while the head and neck are painted on the movable disc. On the movement of the lever the cow is represented very naturally as taking a drink.

CONUNDRUM COMIC SLIDES are similar in construction to trans-formation comic slides. The frame simply carries an opaque plate, in the centre of which an aperture is cut, and on the loose sliding glass is printed a conundrum, and adjoining it the answer. The conundrum being first shown, the answer is seen by pulling out the slide. Figs. 84 and 85 represent the positions during question and answer.

One of the best mechanical comic slides ever invented is Beale's Choreutoscope. It consists of a frame containing one long slide, on which is painted a skeleton in six different positions. In the frame is an aperture, so that one only of the positions can be seen at a time. A handle is so arranged at the back that by turning the same, each position of the skeleton is made to appear alter-nately, and by a very ingenious cam motion the transit from one position to another is performed instantaneously ; also a shutter is caused to close the aperture entirely at the time of transit, thereby preventing the possibility of any one seeing any portion of two positions at once. The effect produced on working the handle is that of a skeleton performing an extempore step dance.

In addition to the *mechanical* comic slides, a variety of humorous ones are now produced, for exhibiting in the ordinary way nursery tales, Æsop's "Fables," and comic stories, as "The Tale of a Tub," "The Fox and the Stork," "The Elephant's Revenge," etc., all conducive to the greatest merriment. Motto Slides, such as "Welcome," "Adieu," "Good night," etc., if judiciously used, give *éclat* to an entertainment.

CHROMO PICTURES.—Messrs. J. Barnard & Son, have published a variety of the above for use in the Magic Lantern. The subjects consist chiefly of Scriptural stories, "Æsop's Fables," natural phenomena, dissolving view effects, and a long list of comic slides. These pictures are printed upon paper in highly brilliant and transparent colours. By using the materials supplied, and keeping to the instructions given, the amateur may soon increase his stock of slides, at a small cost and a little trouble.

VIEWING PICTURES.

Having now considered the different forms of lanterns, with their details and appliances, as well as the various classes of pictures, it may be as well to say a few words as to the most effective way of viewing a lantern exhibition. It must be admitted that however fine a picture or a photograph may be when viewed in the hand, upon being magnified on the screen some two or three thousand times, its defects will be manifest by a near observer, and it is well known that many very beautiful pictures viewed from a distance assume a flat, coarse, and dauby appearance upon closer inspection. Now, by uniting these facts, we arrive at the proper position for viewing : the nearer we are to the screen, the coarser and flatter will the picture be seen, and as we recede, its defects become less apparent; but were we to recede too far, not only would the defects disappear, but also the details, so that under these circumstances the best position for viewing is close to the lantern.

Some attempts have been made to show pictures on the screen in relief, similar to stereoscopic representations, and some experimentalists have actually asserted their success in combining binocular pictures by means of two lanterns. A very little study of binocular vision, or of the stereoscope, will convince any one that such an effect is impossible to produce.

From the introduction in Sir David Brewster's work on the stereoscope, published by Mr. John Murray, the following is extracted :—" When the artist represents living objects, or groups of them, and delineates buildings or landscapes, or when he copies from statues or models, he produces apparent solidity, and difference of distance from the eye, by light and shade, by the diminished size of known objects as regulated by the principles of geometrical perspective, and by the variation in distinctness and colour which constitute what have been called aerial perspective ; but when all the appliances have been used in the most skilful manner, and art has exhausted its powers, we seldom, if ever, mistake the plain . picture for the solid which it represents. The two eyes scan its surface, and by their distance-giving power indicate to the observer that every point of the picture is nearly at the same distance from his eye. But if the observer closes one eye, and thus deprives himself of the power of determining differences of distance by the convergency of the optical axes, the relief of the picture is increased. When the pictures are truthful photographs, in which the variations of light and shade are perfectly represented, a very considerable degree of relief and solidity is thus obtained, and when we have practised for a while this species of monocular vision, the drawing, whether it be a statue, a living figure, or a building, will appear to rise in its different parts from the canvas."

And at page 46 of the same work :—" When we view a picture with both eyes, we discover, from the convergency of the optic axes, that the picture is on a plain surface, every part of which is nearly equidistant from us. But when we shut one eye, we do not make this discovery, and therefore the effect with which the artist gives relief to the painting exercises its whole effect in deceiving us, and hence in monocular vision the 'relievo' of the painting is much more complete."

As this applies equally to the picture on the screen, it is clearly shown that with one eye the best effect is obtained, and the nearer the observer is to the screen, the more important this becomes.

DESCRIPTIVE LECTURES.

WHEN slides can be shown in series, lectures or descriptions of the views should be given, not necessarily a formal lecture, as from the amateur they are more effective when spoken than read. Set lectures are to be purchased, at small cost, on very many subjects, or can be arranged from tourists' guide books, which can be got of the whole world. After all the slides are arranged and numbered in boxes in the order to be shown, each slide should be taken out separately, and the lecturer should now rehearse several times in private his description, with the slides before him, and if needs be, pointing out the places of interest, as he will when the picture is on the screen. Even when slides are not in complete series, and the exhibitor has to make up his entertainment by slides of various places, one or two of London, a few of Paris, Switzerland, Egypt, etc, a description of the views should in all cases be given, for instead of simply calling out " the Pyramids of Egypt," if something can be said of their age, by whom built, and for what their supposed purpose, their size, position, etc., a double interest is given to the picture. It is as well in giving a mixed entertainment, or " Scenes in Many Lands," to keep those belonging to one country together, also those of another, and let the whole be exhibited in something like order, as nothing looks more disorderly than first to be shown a picture in America, then one of Paris, next one of Niagara Falls, etc. A little music will add much to the charm of an exhibition, care being taken that the airs selected should be in keeping with the subjects shown. National airs may be introduced in their proper places with effect, but nothing would appear so ridiculous as to hear the tune of " Johnny comes marching home again," to a picture of " the Return of the Prodigal Son " on the screen.

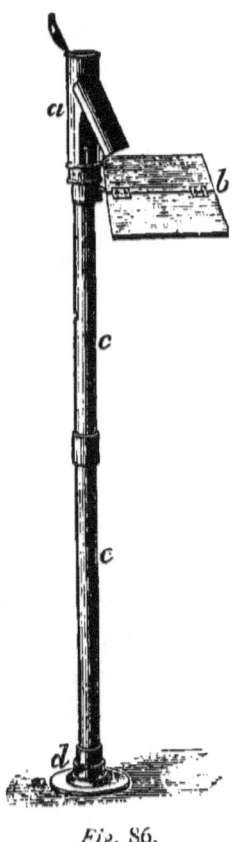

Fig. 86.

READING DESK.

A MOST useful and portable combined Lamp and Reading-Desk is shown in Fig. 86, fitted up for use.

The Lamp is similar to the ordinary railway travellers' carriage reading-lamp, in which standard size candles are used, and which are fitted into a spring socket, so that the flame is always kept at the same level. This lamp A is fixed on the top of a rod C C, which for the convenience of packing is made in two lengths, coupled in the centre by a ferrule. The lower end of the rod is fixed in a brass socket D, which forms a foot; underneath this is a short strong taper screw, by which the whole is fixed to the floor.

The desk is composed of two thin pieces of wood hinged together, as shown, and is attached to the stand by means of a

Fig. 87.

hook and socket just below the lamp, which is also provided with a silvered reflector and an adjusting flap, answering the double purpose of throwing the light on to the desk whilst preventing the light from escaping into the room.

Another Reading Lamp is shown at Fig. 87, which in many respects is superior to that previously described. It is arranged to burn sperm oil, and a screw cap serves as an extinguisher, and prevents the oil from running out when being carried. It is provided with a silent signal at s, and a bell at n if necessary; there is also a match-box fitted at M, the whole packing into a box $3 \times 3 \times 9\frac{1}{2}$ inches.

SCIENTIFIC PROJECTIONS.

IT seems very surprising that the attention of science teachers has not been more given to the Magic Lantern, although latterly many are becoming alive to the importance of its application, for not only can an effect be more clearly shown to a large assembly, but less bulky and less expensive apparatus are needed. Moreover, only one subject being treated at a time, the attention of the student can be more closely concentrated on the one point. It is to be hoped that more consideration may be given to this instrument as a medium for scientific education, and as appliances and apparatus are becoming more general, we may look forward to the time when almost every branch of science may be illustrated by projection, with equal facility and better effect than can be produced at the lecturer's table.

DIAGRAMS,

or Drawings for the illustration of lectures, may be made as follows :—

A piece of glass of usual size for lantern slides is rubbed with tallow, or waxed, then held over the flame of a piece of burning camphor : this will give it a perfectly opaque surface, upon which Diagrams may be drawn, or it may be written upon with a fine point. These, when projected upon the screen in the usual way, have the appearance of chalk drawings upon a black ground. These may be protected by another glass, and made up as an ordinary slide. For copying drawings or diagrams Mr. Woodbury says : "An excellent medium is formed by making a varnish of gum dammar in benzole of the ordinary consistency, and adding a few drops of india-rubber to the same solution. This dries perfectly transparent, and allows of the finest writing to be made upon it by means of a steel pen and Indian-ink. When circles are required, the centres may be obtained for the compasses by damping a piece of card and attaching it, removing same when done with. By coating mica with this, all sorts of designs may be quickly traced from any scientific work."

For a Demonstrative Lantern few are more suitable than the "Sciopticon," which may be used with its powerful oil-burning lamp for small results, or also with the lime-light if necessary.

The slide stage, a portion of which is removable, is most conveniently arranged for the adaptation of most kinds of philosophical appliances; the objectives are easily removed; and the condensers are arranged from the *outside,* thus offering greater facilities than the old style of lantern with the condensers inside.

OPTICAL EXPERIMENTS

may be exhibited: parallel, converging, and diverging rays may be shown by the condensers, and intensity of illumination, refraction, and a variety of optical phenomena are all within its reach.

THE MICROSCOPE

is a valuable attachment to the Magic Lantern. The lenses introduced are of much shorter focus than the ordinary lantern objectives, and the object must be a greater distance from the condenser.

The best position is shown at Fig. 88, c being the condenser, s the slide, and o the objective. The rays emanating from the condenser will cross at the focus, and then diverge, the objective being so placed that all, or as much light as possible, may pass through it. The light may be drawn back so as to obtain the best result. It is most important in using this adaptation that all the parts be central.

When objects are to be shown a large size, enlarged photographs are often used; but these are never so good as originals, being devoid of their natural colours. As most microscopic slides are mounted with Canada balsam, they must not be kept too long in the lantern, or they may be seriously injured by the heat concentrated upon them. To avoid this danger, the best lantern microscropes are provided with alum tanks, through which the

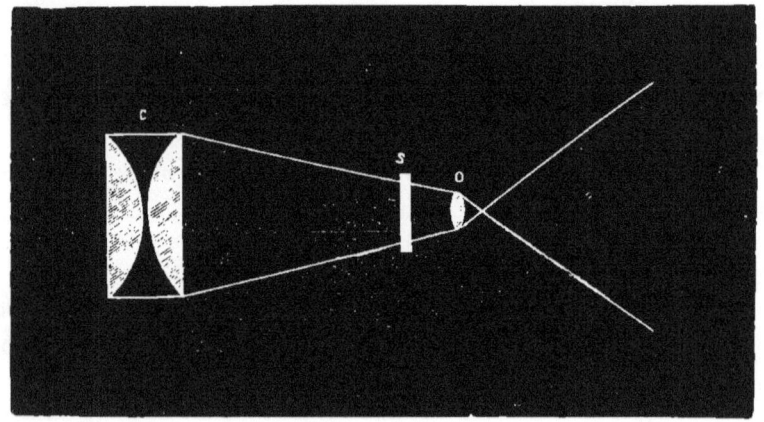

Fig. 88.

light passes previous to reaching the slide, the object of which is to absorb the heat rays. The extent of magnifying power which may be employed is limited by the amount of light obtained in illuminating the object, so very high powers or large discs should not be attempted with anything less than the lime or electric light.

Recently the Lantern Microscope has received much consideration from Mr. Lewis Wright, assisted in the mechanical arrangements by Mr. H. C. Newton, and by their combined efforts a very perfect instrument has been produced, as shown at Fig. 89.

With this instrument screen demonstrations can be given by the oxy-hydrogen lime-light, of a character hitherto quite unattainable. Ample light is obtained for the magnification of ordinarily transparent subjects to 1,250 diameters, which will display in a clear and beautiful manner all the parts of insects, the minute details of anatomical sections, vegetable tissue, &c. A flea may be shown upon the screen, fifteen feet long, quite as sharply, and almost as brilliantly, as a magic lantern slide; the proboscis of a

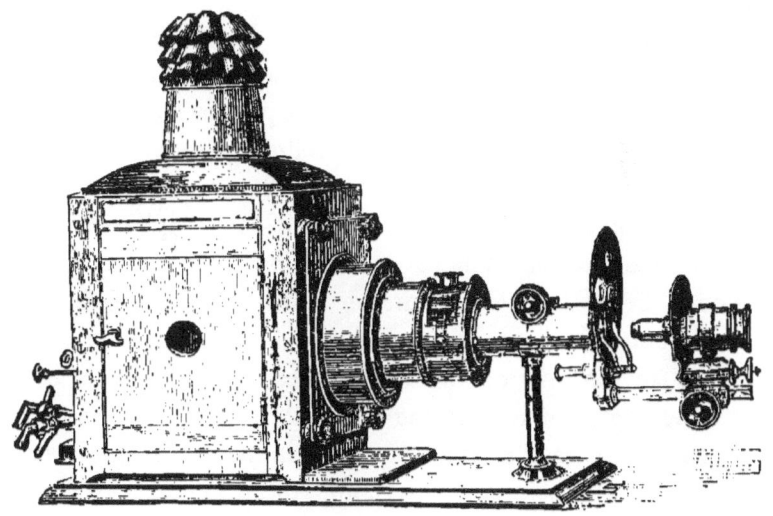

Fig. 89.

blow-fly is easily displayed with the various powers from eight to fourteen feet long; and all the details of an insect's eye are shown in section clearly. The circulation of the blood is easily displayed in the veins of the living frog, and pond life is of course shown without any difficulty. Where transparency of ground is combined with opacity of detail, as in the cornea of a fly's eye, a magnification of 2,500 diameters is obtainable. Geological sections are admirably shown either by ordinary or *polarized light.*

The microscope can be fitted to any good optical lantern. In the special lantern constructed for use with the instrument, a triple 5-in. primary condenser is used, similar to that shown at Fig. 4, which takes up the large angle of 95° of light from the radiant. Almost equal results can, however, be obtained with the 4-in. condensers usually supplied in optical lanterns, by the addition of a third lens; the triple 5-in. condenser being reckoned to give 15 per cent. more illumination.

During the Franco-Prussian War, when Paris was in a state of siege, and communication with the outer world deemed an impossibility, despatches and copies of newspapers were, by means of micro-photographs upon thin films of collodion, carried by pigeons to the interior of the capital. These films, which were about 2 inches long by 1 inch wide, contained each copies of sixteen pages of despatches, each page consisting of 5,000 letters, the reduction being the eight-hundredth part of the size of the original. Twenty of these despatches could be carried in a quill attached to the tails of these novel postmen. As soon as the despatches were received at the telegraph office, they were placed between two plates of glass and inserted in the microscope lantern, the electric light being employed, and the characters were reproduced of sufficient size to be read and copied with ease. An illustration of this forms our Frontispiece.

Objects suitable to the lantern microscope are whole insects, butterflies, wood sections, and fine crystals of many chemicals, such as sulphate of copper, sulphate of iron, chloride of ammonium, chloride of barium, alum, camphor dissolved in water, etc. A variety of tank experiments also may be introduced, as the animalculæ in water, suitable water for examination being found in stagnant pools, or water in which flowers or hay have been standing for some few days. A very pretty effect may be witnessed of the formation of crystals if a slip of glass be wetted with a strong solution of Epsom salts, and then placed in the microscope. In a short time the water will evaporate from the upper edge, and crystallization will at once begin; if too slowly, it may be hastened by blowing upon the surface of the slip; very soon the screen will be covered with a representation of a beautiful crystalline formation. A most convenient screen for exhibiting microscopic objects may be made by tracing-paper, stretched on a youth's wooden hoop, as described at page 87.

THE OXY-HYDROGEN POLARISCOPE.

This is an instrument with which one of the most interesting branches of science can be studied. To attempt an explanation of the remarkable phenomena of polarized light is entirely out of the limits of this treatise, therefore we will content ourselves with a description and method of applying the instrument. The peculiar properties called polarization may be imparted to light in various methods of refraction and reflection.

It is about forty years ago that Mr. J. F. Goddard received the silver medal of the Society of Arts for his invention of the "Oxy-hydrogen Polariscope," illustrated at Fig. 90. Thus described:—

" In this instrument A represents the oxy-hydrogen blow-pipe, B the lime-cylinder, and diverging rays of light refracted by the con densing lens c c c, and falling upon a mirror B B, consisting of plates of flattened crown glass placed in the elbow of a tube, bent to the polarizing angle of crown glass; D, converging rays of polarized light reflected from the mirror; H H, a bundle of sixteen plates of mica for analysing the light previously polarized by reflection; E, a double-reflecting crystal (film of selenite), placed in focus of the object glass (I), which forms an image of the crystal upon a disc or screen at R. As the analysing bundle of mica is caused to

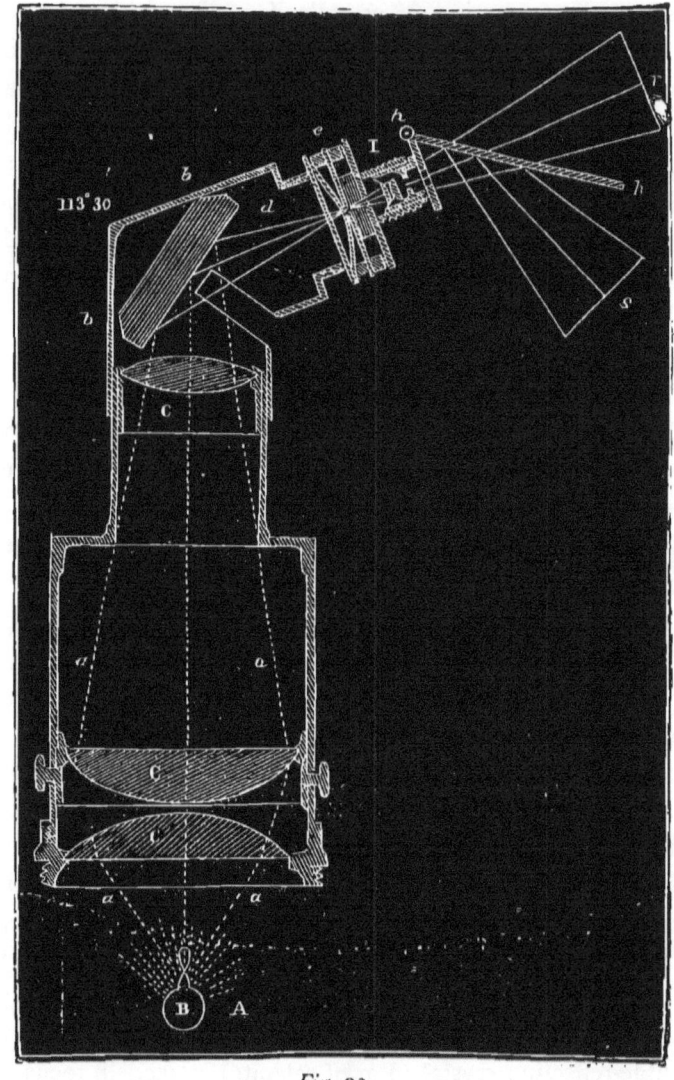

Fig. 92.

revolve, the image of the selenite upon the disc undergoes all the
change, and exhibits alternately the primary and complementary

colours at the same time, one being reflected in the direction s, and the other transmitted and seen at R. The great advantage of polarizing the light from a number of plates is, that a beam of any required dimension can be obtained, also of much greater intensity than by any other means ; for whatever single surface may be employed, that polarized light at the same angle as the glass used (which for crown glass is 56 45), we obtain an additional quantity by laying upon it a single plate of such glass, and a further quantity by the addition of a second, third, or any further number. The quantity of light added by each succeeding plate being, however, less in proportion to the number of plates through which it has to pass. In this respect the single-image Nichol's prism of Iceland Spar is decidedly the best for analysing, as by this a great variety of objects may be exhibited." This latter Nichol's prism analyser is, therefore, most generally used, being mounted in a tube by which it may be revolved in front of the objectives, the subjects for examination being placed in the rays of polarized light, between the mirror or polarizer and the objective. From the optical instrument makers may be obtained transparent butterflies, flowers, and other objects made from thin films of crystals, of selenite, or mica, and when these are placed in the polariscope, the most brilliant variations of colour are projected on the screen as the analyser is made to revolve.[*]

THE SPECTRUM,

or Dispersion of Light, and also Spectrum Analysis, may be fairly conducted by the oxy-hydrogen lantern, but for the latter purpose a special kind of jet is required. To show the Spectrum by means of the lantern, perhaps no way is more effective than that of the

---

[*] See " Light," a Course of Experimental Optics, by Lewis Wright.

rainbow as an effect upon a landscape picture, or upon such a view as Niagara Falls. To accomplish this a second lantern is indispensable, one for the view, the other for the rainbow. The view

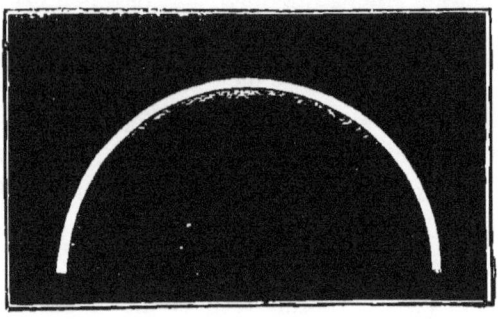

Fig. 91.

is shown on the screen by the one lantern in the usual manner. A piece of sheet brass or tin, in which is cut a semicircular slit, as shown at Fig. 91, is next placed in the second lantern, thereby

Fig. 92.

projecting a semicircle of white light. A prism must now be placed in front of the objective, which will cause the semicircle of white light to leave the screen, and probably on the floor or the ceiling it would be seen, but not as before, for by the introduction of the prism the light would be decomposed, and present a fair illustration of the colours of the rainbow. The lantern must now be raised in front so as to bring the effect on the screen into its proper position, as at Fig. 92. It is often more convenient to turn the lantern sideways than to elevate it in front, and by using the prism in a vertical position an equally good effect can be obtained, but a larger prism is rendered necessary.

THE KALEIDOSCOPE.

This instrument, the invention of Sir David Brewster, has been for years before the public, and is almost an universal favourite. Its

Fig. 93.

adaptation to the lantern has been accomplished, notwithstanding very many difficulties. Mr. Darker, of Lambeth, has devoted much time and attention to this adaptation, and that exhibited at the Royal Polytechnic was of his manufacture. It may be briefly described thus : A pair of plain mirrors, fixed inside a brass tube, at each extremity of which is placed a lens, the one placed nearest the lantern condenser being a meniscus, and at the other end being plano convex.   In other words, it forms a lantern objective, with two plain mirrors inserted in the position of a V between the lenses. The light must be raised above the centre of the condensers, and upon the proper adjustment of the light and the exact centring of the optical arrangements its success much depends.   This instrument cannot be used in connection with the lantern with any satisfactory result, except by lime light, and even then to no large size.   One great difficulty is experienced by the collection of moisture upon the plain mirrors, which greatly detracts from a perfect illumination.   In the Kaleidoscope sometimes a third reflecting mirror is employed, a cross section of the three forming an equilateral triangle. A pattern or design produced by such an arrangement is shown at Fig. 93.   Various substances may be introduced to produce different effects, such as broken coloured glass, pins, needles, etc., which can be inserted by removing the meniscus lens from the tube.

TOTAL REFLECTION.

The "Illuminated Cascade" will well repay the trouble of its production.   This effect was shown some years ago at the Royal Polytechnic Institution, where Mons. Duboscq, of Paris, erected a very elaborate arrangement, the exhibition causing universal admiration.   To exhibit this effect on a small scale, the apparatus necessary consists of a tall glass vessel, supported on a stand, and placed in front of the condenser, the objectives being removed.   An illustration is given at Fig. 94.   The vessel A must be wholly covered with black paper, except at c, where the rays of light from the condenser enter, and are brought to a focus at B, which is a circular orifice, from which a stream of water issues in the form shown; the rays of light, being carried with it, are reflected from side to side of the arched column of water, which is illuminated in a most lovely manner through its course. If various coloured glasses be inserted

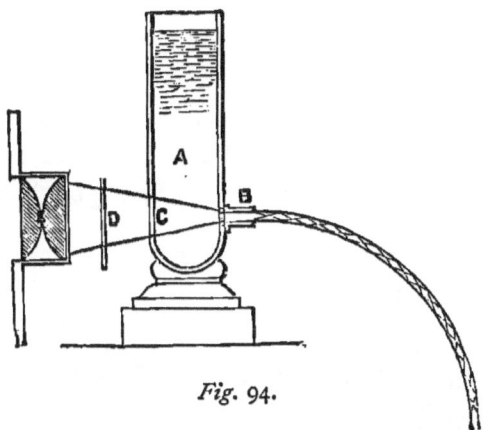

Fig. 94.

at D, the effect produced is still more beautiful. To insure success, the orifice B should be perfectly round and smooth, allowing the stream to issue unbroken; and when adding more water, it must be done very quietly, so as not to cause a current, or the effect will be lost.

An experiment illustrating the

REFRACTION OF GLASS

may be shown as follows:—After preparing a glass plate with burning camphor, as previously described, draw upon it a line or an arrow about 2 inches in length. This, upon being inserted in the lantern, will show a white line or arrow upon the dark ground. Now take a strip of glass about ½ inch broad and ¼ thick, insert it in front of the slide at right angles to the arrow or line: so long as it is kept at right angles, no refraction will be seen; but on inclining it so that the rays of light shall pass through it obliquely, a piece of the arrow or line will appear to be cut out and moved to one side : the thicker the glass the greater the displacement.

THE PERSISTENCE OF VISION

may be illustrated by a little instrument styled a Kaleidotrope. It consists of a disc of tin perforated, as shown in Fig. 95, attached to the wood block by means of a lateral spiral spring, being free to revolve upon its centre point. When projected on the screen nothing more is seen than a number of white spots, but upon giving

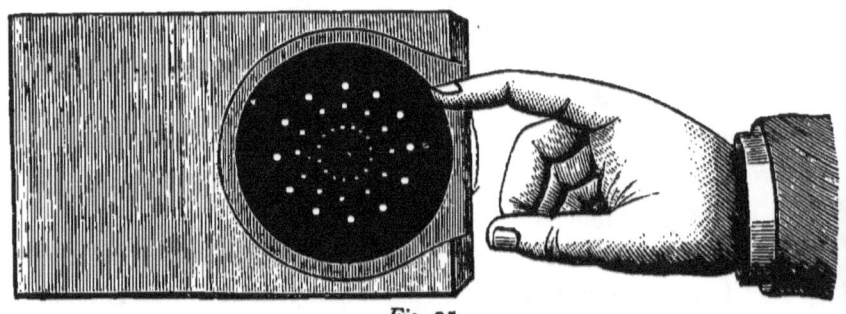

Fig. 95.

motion to the disc by a touch of the finger, circles of light are seen beautifully interlacing one another. The principle is that of " Persistence of Vision," and may be compared to the boyish experiment of whirling round a lighted stick, and so causing an apparent circle of light.

COLOUR EXPERIMENTS

form a most interesting branch of science, and are easily conducted by means of the Magic Lantern. A series of such experiments were published some time ago by Mr. W. B. Woodbury, from which the following are extracted. Two discs of thin cardboard are obtained, in each of which must be cut three circular apertures. Three pieces of different coloured gelatine are now attached to the backs of each disc, a yellow piece covering one aperture, a red the second aperture, and a blue piece the third; so that upon looking through the disc it will present three circles, one red, one blue, and one yellow. Should these discs be placed in a chromatrope-holder, and made to revolve in opposite directions, the secondary colours will, of course, be seen (Fig. 96). "But great care must be taken, in choosing the blue, to

Fig. 96.

see that it is not of a purple tint, otherwise no approach to a green will be obtained. On attaching two discs to one circle and

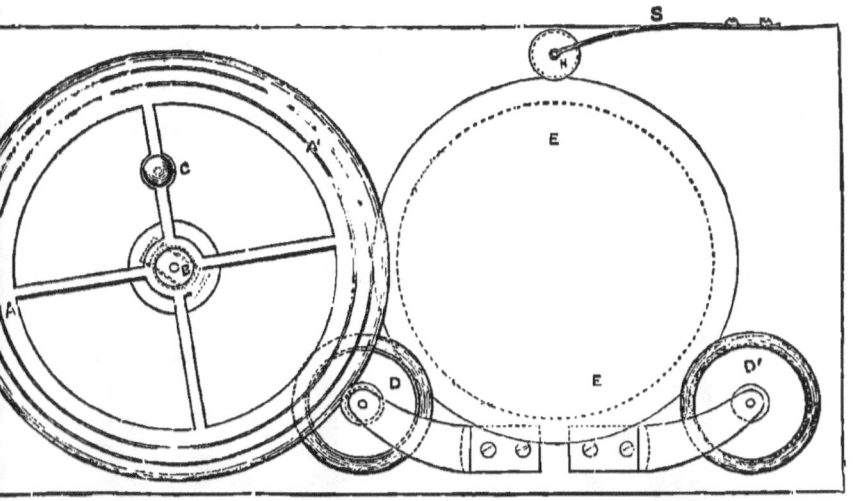

Fig. 97.

one to the other, the red being over the blue in the first, we then get all the tertiary colours."

An instrument, called the Chromodrome, illustrated at Fig. 97, is arranged for communicating rapid motion to discs of glass, which have various designs attached in coloured gelatine. At Fig. 98 we have a design which will give all the delicate gradations of any colour mixed with white tints in steps, whilst Fig. 99 will give a continual graduated tint. A series of thirty different designs, and a short Manual, by Mr. John Gorham, on the Rudiments of Colour by Rotation," together with an apparatus for rotating the designs, is supplied by A. N. Myers & Co., London. All these may be copied, and exhibited to a large audience by means of the lantern, with great effect.

Another striking way of showing complementary colours is by

  means of a set of slides manu-factured by the Sciopticon Company, and consist of sheets of perforated zinc, mounted with sheets of coloured gelatine between glass plates, together with a duplicate design without

Fig. 98.   *Fig.* 99.

the coloured gelatine. Two of these are shown at Figs. 100 and 101.

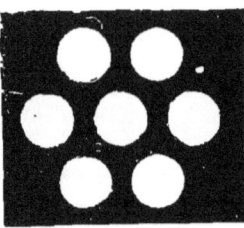

Fig. 100.   *Fig.* 101.

CHEMICAL EXPERIMENTS.

Most of the chemical experiments usually shown before classes can be conducted in the lantern with great success, but for this purpose it is necessary that the slide stage shall be open at the top. A tank will be necessary, which may be made of two plates of white glass, kept apart by a strip of india-rubber about half an inch thick, bent round their sides and secured by four screw clamps. Such a tank will hold almost any kind of solution, and is very accessible for cleaning. A neater apparatus, is shown at Fig. 102. A few pipettes will also be required. These may be made of pieces of glass tube, one end of which should be drawn to a fine point;

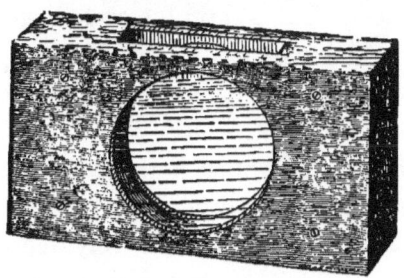

Fig. 102.

or a useful pipette, shown at Fig. 103, may be obtained, provided with an elastic ball. The experiments which come under the above head are so numerous that only a few will here be given.

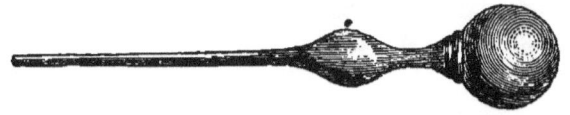

Fig. 103.

Part fill the tank with water, and add a solution of litmus, till the whole becomes of a bluish-purple tint; now by dropping into it from the pipette very dilute acid, a cloudlike effect is produced, and ultimately the whole becomes red. Now, if dilute ammonia be added in like manner, a change is brought about, and the original colour is restored.

Fill the tank with dilute alcohol, and add drop by drop of almost any of the aniline colours (Judson's dyes). The effect resembles a tree shooting out in a variety of ways and branches; and by using different colours at the sides and centre the effect is wonderfully increased.

The Silver Tree is produced by partly filling the tank with a dilute solution of nitrate of silver. A piece of copper is now bent into the form of an arc, and allowed to dip into the solution. It should now be nicely focussed on the screen, and in a very short time pure silver will be deposited on the copper wire in arborescent form, varying in form in proportion to the strength of the solution.

Precipitation may be shown with the same solution as used in the silver tree experiment, by dropping from the pipette into the solution dilute hydrochloric acid, when very dense clouds of chloride of silver will be produced, which will ultimately subside to the bottom of the tank. By adding strong ammonia, the precipitate will be re-dissolved, and the solution become clear.

Crystallization of many substances is well worthy of notice. Thus, if a saturated solution of sulphate of soda be placed in the tank, and a crystal of the same added, the whole will shoot out into a mass of beautiful crystals.

PHOTOGRAPHY.

The development of the photographic image is always a fascinating experiment, and may be performed without much trouble in the following manner: In the first place, the room mnst be in perfect darkness, with the exception of the light of a candle filtered through a sheet of coloured gelatine or ruby glass. A strip of glass, say 4¼ by 2 inches, or half a quarter-plate cut lengthways, is better for experiment than a larger plate, as, the edges being in view when the picture begins to develop, the effect is better observed. A thin solution of india-rubber in benzole or chloroform should now be applied to the edges of the glass plate; this will dry almost instantaneously. Now coat the glass with a collodion emulsion, better procured ready prepared. As soon as set, it may be dried over a spirit lamp, and is then ready for printing. One end of the glass plate must now be marked, or if the emulsion be kept a little from one end, this will serve to distinguish it after printing. This precaution is necessary so as to prevent the possibility of developing the picture upside down. It must now be placed in *contact* with a sharp negative, face to face the length way, crossing the negative and the marked end of the prepared plate at the bottom. It may be held in position in an ordinary pressure printing-frame, and exposed to the light of the lantern, or ordinary gaslight. The exposure will vary with the nature of the light and the density of the negative. (See instructions for printing photographic transparencies, page 92.)

So soon as printed and the light lowered, except the non-actinic light above mentioned, it may be taken from the printing-frame. Now flow over its surface a solution of water and alcohol in equal proportions, and after wash the plate in a cup of water. For the *development*, a tank must be used, with a piece of ruby glass inserted between it and the condenser, and upon turning up the light of the lantern, a ruby disc will be projected on to the screen. If the plate be now placed in the tank (the marked end at the top or outside), no image will be visible. A clear solution of pyrogallic acid and water, three grains to one ounce, is now poured into the tank until it is three parts full, and still no change will be apparent; but upon the application of a few drops of a solution of ammonia and bromide of potassium—

$$\left.\begin{array}{lll} \text{Liquid ammonia} & . & . \quad \text{1 drachm,} \\ \text{Water} & . & . \quad \text{1 ounce,} \\ \text{Bromide potassium} & . & . \quad \text{20 grains,} \\ \text{Water} & . & . \quad \text{1 ounce,} \end{array}\right\} \begin{array}{l} \text{mixed in equal} \\ \text{proportions,} \end{array}$$

the image will gradually appear and very soon acquire sufficient intensity, when it must be removed and washed in a cup of clean water. Another tank is next placed in the lantern without the ruby glass, and nearly filled with a solution of hyposulphite of soda. The plate is now inserted, when it will immediately become clear and more transparent. It should be now removed and washed, and dried over a spirit lamp, when it may be shown as any other transparency.

CAPILLARY ATTRACTION

is shown by a tank (Fig. 102) placed in the lantern, and half filled with water coloured with a few drops of writing ink, so that it will be more clearly seen. Now, by inserting small glass

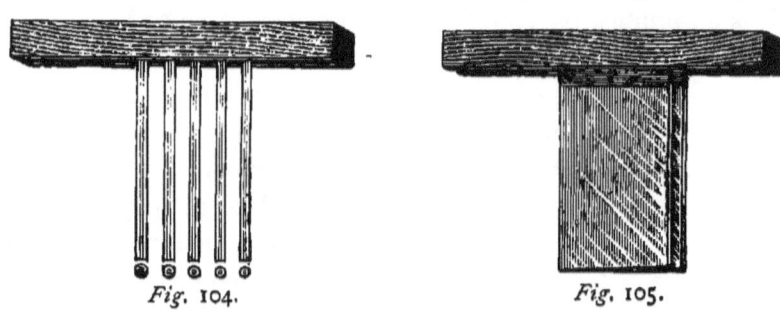

Fig. 104.   Fig. 105.

tubes vertically, the solution will rise inside the tubes in proportion to their diameter. Should a series of glass tubes of different diameters, and arranged in a line on a piece of wood, be inserted (see Fig. 104), the different heights will be clearly shown on the screen, proportionately with the fineness of the tubes. A striking illustration may be shown by means of two glass plates attached to a bar of wood, so that two of the edges touch each other, and the other two are some ¼ inch apart (Fig. 105). When these plates are inserted in the tank, the coloured water will rise between the plates where they are in contact, and slope away with a beautiful curve as the plates become more distant.

EBULLITION.

To illustrate that liquids in the spheroidal state and the metal plate are not in contact, accurately level a smooth flat strip of metal about midway across the condensers so that it can be removed and replaced easily. It must now be heated by a spirit lamp or other convenient method, and replaced, when a few drops of water may be dropped from a pipette upon the hot plate; the water will now assume the spheroidal state, and by means of a fine platinum wire passed into the globule, the liquid may be kept in position, and upon focussing this accurately on the screen, a space will be distinctly seen between the globule and the hot plate.

ELECTRICITY

is another branch of science which can be illustrated by means of the lantern, and with small, simple, and inexpensive apparatus fitted to the lanterns, many experiments can be exhibited to large audiences, which would be almost impracticable to illustrate in any other way, except at a great cost. The apparatus being small, great battery power is seldom required. The bichromate battery offers the best facility to the lecturer: this may be separate, of usual form, or it may be for convenience and portability fitted to the Sciopticon, as is the one in use by the writer, which was devised and constructed by Mr. W. Watts. It is fitted into the hollow space in the lower portion of the front of the Sciopticon, and consists of two cells 5 inches long by 2½ inches wide. The outside casing is made of zinc plates, forming a box, each pole of the battery terminating in a slight projecting spring, so that when the battery is put into its place these springs press against two brass studs, which project a little inside the Sciopticon base, and being screwed through the base from the outside, have each soldered on to them, in a vertical position, a split tube similar to a penholder socket. The terminals, which are screwed to the exhibiting tank-frame, being each provided with a brass leg, the tank has only to be pushed down into its place, each leg sliding into its respective socket, and the connections are complete. Should it be desirable to reverse the poles, as in some instances is necessary, this can be done in a moment by simply withdrawing the exhibiting tank from its sockets and reversing its position. As this battery holds only a small quantity of solution, it will not keep up an energetic action so long as the conventional bulbous form of battery, but it possesses for lantern requirements sufficient lasting power, also the feature of compactness and portability dispensing with wires, which are liable to be pulled out or become entangled in the dark.

The solution cannot be spilt, as the battery is provided with suitable lid and india-rubber pad, also two thumb-screws which effectually tighten all down and prevent any leakage.

The lantern being no more bulky with this attachment than without it, and consequently requiring no extra packing, together with its extreme facility for manipulation, make it very desirable and useful attachment.

ELECTRO DEPOSITION.

The deposition of one metal upon another by electricity or magnetism—almost invariably the more precious metals being deposited upon the baser—has of late years become so extended as to assume the proportions of a large and lucrative trade, divided into several branches: enormous quantities of nickel and copper, thousands of ounces of silver and gold, besides numerous other metals, are being consumed annually in the various processes of electro deposition. Scarcely a trade exists in which this useful art is not connected in some way or other, from the massive copper-covered roller of the calico printer, to the most elaborate and costly works of art; and faithful copies of the most antique works of the ancients are being constantly reproduced by those firms who have made this branch of the art their speciality. It cannot, therefore, but be interesting to some of our readers to see and learn something of this important branch of industry, which came into existence about the same period as its sister-art, photography: the one owing its principle of action to light, the other to electricity or magnetism; both illustrating some of the most wonderful of nature's phenomena.

It is in this as in other portions of this work neither our *forte* nor intention to attempt an exhaustive treatise upon this subject, our desire being simply to direct the attention of the student by as brief a description as a clear explanation will admit, to a few interesting experiments, projected on the screen, illustrative of electro deposition.

For this purpose a tank and battery will be required: the tank should have two brass terminals, one screwed into each side at the top of the wood frame, to receive the wires from the battery, the most convenient form of which is the bichromate; this should be at least a pint in capacity. Next procure about four grains of fine gold, rolled very thin, about the size of a postage-stamp, also a piece of copper gauze about the same size; this should be flattened a little with a hammer, to close up the texture. Both the gauze and gold plate must have now a piece of thin copper wire, about 4 inches long, soldered to their respective edges; then twist up the free ends into a loop, and screw up tight between the terminals and wood frame. The wires may now be bent, so as to let the gold plate or anode, and copper gauze or cathode, occupy the centre of the tank without touching each other. Now nearly fill the tank with water, and drop into it a piece of cyanide of potassium, about the size of a horse-bean; whilst it is dissolving, connect up the battery by attaching the wire from the carbon plate to the gold terminal, and the wire from the zinc plate to the copper terminal; lower the zinc plate into the battery solution, and electrolysis will commence immediately. If the anode and cathode or electrodes, as we will now call them, have been adjusted parallel to each other, they can be accurately focussed upon the screen : the image will now appear as a large black square and a trelliswork side by side; and if the battery power be brisk, globules of hydrogen will be evolved from the anode with great rapidity, very shortly the edges of which will become frayed; and as the action goes on a number of perforations will gradually extend from the edges to the centre of the plate; and as it becomes more diaphanous through the continued action, the peculiar texture or crystalline perforations will be more easily observed; and, as the action is still further continued, these perforations will gradually enlarge until small particles of the anode will become detached and fall to the bottom of the tank. While this is going on with the anode, the spaces in the cathode are as gradually becoming filled up; and if the action be allowed to proceed indefinitely, the cathode, or a portion of it, will become so filled up as to almost entirely prevent the transmission of light, whilst the anode will disappear altogether. The liquid in the tank will now have become formed into a double cyanide of gold, but it will only have a small quantity of gold suspended in the solution; because, almost as fast as it can be dissolved from the anode, it will become deposited upon the cathode. This deposit will be of a brownish-yellow colour, it being necessary to raise the temperature of the solution to about 140 degrees to produce the proper gold colour of deposit. This could readily be done by the aid of a spirit lamp, and by observing a few other chemical conditions; but, as this would not improve the effect of the chemical action upon the screen, we may as well dispense with the extra trouble, our object being to utilize for our purpose only those effects which the transmission of light will demonstrate.

Magnetic and diamagnetic phenomena may be demonstrated by use of a small electro magnet, shown attached to a light wood frame at Fig. 106. The magnet should be of soft common iron, with a hole, as shown in the illustration, through which articles to

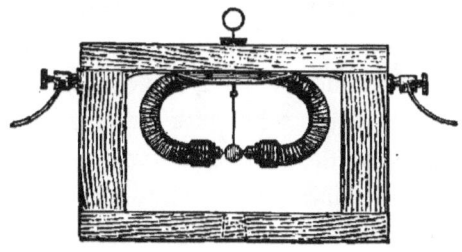

Fig. 106.

be operated upon may be passed. The frame is to be placed in the lantern and the poles of the magnet focussed upon the screen, and with a small battery power some very interesting effects may be illustrated. Fine iron filings, if dropped gently through the hole at the top between the poles, will attach themselves to each pole and give a very curious outline on the screen, increasing in size as the filings are dropped through, until at length they meet together and form the magnetic curve. By fitting into the hole of the frame a cork, through which a brass wire is made to pass, needles and other small articles may be suspended by a silk thread. In the illustration a small disc is shown suspended in the manner described. When a needle or iron disc is suspended between the poles of the magnet, being attracted by them, it takes up a position of rest, joining the poles as illustrated; but a rod or disc of bismuth, on the other hand, would be repelled by the poles of the magnet, and would take up its position of rest at right angles to the poles, thus placing themselves equatorially and illustrating diamagnetism. Pieces of iron, copper, alum, sulphur, paper, charcoal, and small tubes filled with various solutions, such as those of iron, cobalt, water, alcohol, etc., etc., are all suitable for suspending and operating upon.

The electro decomposition of water is effected by sending a current of electricity from three or four cells through water slightly acidulated by sulphuric acid. Through the bottom of the tank two platinum wires should be fixed, projecting some distance into the solution; two test-tubes filled with the acidulated water should now be introduced into the tank, one standing over each platinum terminal, which will thus project into the tubes say $\frac{3}{4}$ inch: as soon as the current of electricity is caused to pass, from these wires, bubbles will be seen to rise, and soon one test-tube will be filled with hydrogen gas, the other, in which oxygen will be present, will only be half full in the same time.

THE END.

DALZIEL BROTHERS, CAMDEN PRESS, LONDON, N W.

Late Publications of Scovill Manufacturing Co., New York.

SCOVILL'S PHOTO. SERIES.

TO MAKE PHOTOGRAPHS, containing full instructions for making Paper Negatives. (One hundred and twenty thousand.) Sent free to any practitioner of the art.

No. 1 —THE PHOTOGRAPHIC AMATEUR. By J. Traill Taylor. A Guide to the Young Photographer, either Professional or Amateur. (Second Ed.) $0 50

No. 2.—THE ART AND PRACTICE OF SILVER PRINTING. (Second Edition) 50

No. 3.—Out of print.

No. 4.—HOW TO MAKE PICTURES.—Third edition. The A B C of Dry-Plate Photography. By Henry Clay Price. Illuminated Cover, 50 cts.; Cloth Cover 75

No. 5.—PHOTOGRAPHY WITH EMULSIONS. By Capt. W. De W. Abney, R.E., F.R.S. A treatise on the theory and practical working of Gelatine and Collodion Emulsion Processes 1 00

No. 6.—No. 17 has taken the place of this book.

No. 7.—THE MODERN PRACTICE OF RETOUCHING —As practiced by M. Piquepé, and other celebrated experts. (Second Edition)...... 25

No. 8.—THE SPANISH EDITION OF HOW TO MAKE PICTURES.—Ligeras Lecciones sobre Fotografía Dedicados a Los Aficionados.................... 1 00

No. 9. -TWELVE ELEMENTARY LESSONS IN PHOTOGRAPHIC CHEM- ISTRY.- Presented in very concise and attractive shape... 25

No. 10.—THE BRITISH JOURNAL PHOTOGRAPHIC ALMANAC FOR 1883. 25

No. 11.—Out of print.

No. 12.—HARDWICH'S CHEMISTRY.—A manual of photographic chemistry, theoretical and practical. Ninth Edition. Edited by J. Traill Taylor, $2.00 ; Cloth.. 2 50

No 13.—TWELVE ELEMENTARY LESSONS ON SILVER PRINTING. No 2 has taken the place of this book.

No. 14.—ABOUT PHOTOGRAPHY AND PHOTOGRAPHERS.—A series of in- teresting essays for the studio and study, to which is added European Rambles with a Camera. By H. Baden Pritchard, F.C.S 50

No. 15.—THE CHEMICAL EFFECT OF THE SPECTRUM. By Dr. J. M. Eder 25

No. 16.—PICTURE MAKING BY PHOTOGRAPHY. By H. P. Robinson. Author of Pictorial Effect in Photography. Written in popular form and finely illustrated. Illuminated Cover, 75 cts.; Cloth 1 00

No. 17.—FIRST LESSONS IN AMATEUR PHOTOGRAPHY. By Prof. Ran- dall Spaulding. A series of popular lectures, giving elementary instruc- tion in dry-plate photography, optics, etc....... 25

No. 18.—THE STUDIO: AND WHAT TO DO IN IT. By H. P. Robinson. Author of Pictorial Effect in Photography, Picture Making by Photog- raphy, etc.; Illuminated Cover. 75

No. 19.—THE MAGIC LANTERN MANUAL. (Second edition.) By W. I. Chadwick. With one hundred and five practical illustrations ; cloth...... 75

THE BRITISH JOURNAL ALMANAC, AND THE PHOTO. NEWS YEAR- BOOK OF PHOTOGRAPHY FOR 1886. For the two............... 75

ART RECREATION —A guide to decorative art. Ladies' popular guide to home decorative work. Edited by Marion Kemble 2 00

THE FERROTYPER'S GUIDE.—Cheap and complete. For the ferrotyper, this is the only standard work Seventh thousand 75

THE PHOTOGRAPHIC STUDIOS OF EUROPE.—By H. Baden Pritchard, F.C.S. Paper, 50 cts. ; Cloth 1 00

HOW TO MAKE PHOTOGRAPHS (One Hundred Thousand) gratis. Sent free to any practitioner of the art.

WILSON'S PHOTOGRAPHIC PUBLICATIONS.

PHOTOGRAPHIC REFERENCE BOOKS.

www.ingramcontent.com/pod-product-compliance
Lightning Source LLC
Chambersburg PA
CBHW021127020726
47500CB00003B/956